LARGE PRINT SMI
Smith, Rosemary A.
The amethyst brooch

SEP 1 1 2005

JUN - 2 2005

THE AMETHYST BROOCH

In 1873, Jane Merriock travels to Cornwall to visit Pendenna Reach, her mother's childhood home. There she meets for the first time her grandmother, her Aunt Laura and the attractive estate manager, Robert Thornton. But many questions were to be answered. Why were Aunt Laura and Granny Merriock so hostile towards her, and why was Robert Thornton so intent on finding a priest-hole at Pendenna? What did Nora Blackstone know, and who was Jason Trehaine? And why was she so drawn to her mother's beautiful amethyst brooch?

ROSEMARY A. SMITH

THE AMETHYST BROOCH

Complete and Unabridged

LINFORD
Leicester

First published in Great Britain in 2004

First Linford Edition
published 2005

British Library CIP Data

Smith, Rosemary A.
  The amethyst brooch.—Large print ed.—
Linford romance library
  1. Love stories
  2. Large type books
  I. Title
  823.9′2 [F]

ISBN 1–84395–752–3

Published by
F. A. Thorpe (Publishing)
Anstey, Leicestershire

Set by Words & Graphics Ltd.
Anstey, Leicestershire
Printed and bound in Great Britain by
T. J. International Ltd., Padstow, Cornwall

This book is printed on acid-free paper

Dedicated to my dear Dad,
George Broadest, sadly departed.
Thank you for believing in me.

1

I arrived at my mother's childhood home, Pendenna Reach, one afternoon in late September, 1873. I'd come with some trepidation, and as I sat in the carriage waiting for the tall, black, wrought-iron gates to be opened, I thought of the circumstances which had brought me from London to Cornwall in such a short space of time.

I thought back to the day, only three weeks ago, when I sat in the apartments of my godmother, Amy Godbeares, in fashionable Grosvenor Square. The letter from my maternal grandmother lay before me on the table. I'd read it through several times, noting the neat, sloping handwriting, and the slight shake of hand with which it had been written. It had come to me from Pendenna Reach, at the beginning of September.

Dear Jane

You will be somewhat surprised to hear from me, but I have followed your progress through life with love and great interest. I am getting older and have a great sadness in my heart. It would please me so much if you would come to stay at Pendenna for a while, to allow us to get to know one another. Your grandfather passed from the world a year ago and since then I have thought a lot of the past, and wish to redeem in some small way the wrong accorded to your mother, my daughter, Felicity.

Think on this request, my child, and I look forward with anticipation to your reply.

Your loving Grandmother,
Harriet Pendenna.

I rose from my seat and walked to the window looking out over the square. Since my father and mother died of influenza three years ago, Amy had taken me under her wing. I was very happy here, but knew that at the age of twenty I should be looking to my future. Was this a chance to explore new horizons? My mother had often talked of Pendenna Reach, of the rambling corridors and the sea beyond the house.

She'd also told me how, at the age of eighteen, she'd eloped with my father, an artist, to Paris and married him. It all sounded very romantic to me as a girl, but as I grew I sensed sadness in my mother and knew she yearned to see her old home.

My grandfather had disowned her for thwarting him, and had never forgiven her for marrying beneath her. As it turned out, my father became a very successful artist, and the name of John Merriock became famous for his landscape paintings, even more so after his untimely death. I had the consolation of knowing Mama and Papa were always happy together. I had wanted for nothing and after their death had gone to a finishing school for young ladies in Paris.

Amy had been my rock since returning to London a year ago. She'd launched me into Society where I'd met countless young men but none appealed to me. They were all far too shallow and one very much like another. I had definite views on the husband I envisaged, a man strong of character and one who would stand out in a crowd. So, much to Amy's chagrin, I did not succumb to the elegant men I met.

My parents' house near the Thames Embankment, where Papa loved to paint, was sold. I had no desire to keep it on, apart from the fact I could not have afforded its upkeep. So I was left with a useful inheritance to be gained at the age of twenty-one, Mama's personal possessions still under lock and key in a mahogany chest, Molly our housemaid who had learned many new skills under Amy's roof, and my memories.

I picked up Grandmother's letter and made my way to my room. Looking at my reflection in the mirror I thought how much like Mama I looked. My dark brown hair was drawn back in a chignon, one or two tendrils escaping each side of my oval face. I was slim and tall with blue eyes. The pink striped, high-neck blouse I wore, and grey skirt with a small train, made me look even taller. I'd made up my mind, a quick, positive decision, so like me.

I'd go to Pendenna, partly because I felt I owed it to my mother. Also, to know my family would be a new experience. It had always been just the three of us, as Papa's family had sailed to America and settled there, so I never knew them either. But to have a family at this time in my life could only be a good thing, and hopefully give me some direction. Little did I know then what direction my life would take in such a short time.

When Molly came to dress my hair for dinner that evening, a skill she'd acquired from Amy's personal maid, I broached the subject of going to Cornwall.

'Will you come with me, Molly?'

'I'd go to the ends of the earth with you,' she replied immediately.

I was delighted she felt this way, for Molly had been part of my life since I was ten years of age. She was five years my senior and I knew she would be a good companion, but also I knew we both had a lot to learn, as we were both so used to City life.

After two weeks of packing, various farewells to friends and acquaintances, and a tearful goodbye from Amy with a promise to write, Molly and I arrived at Paddington Station for the ten-hour journey to Penzance, where, my grandmother assured me, someone would meet us.

We were amazed at the size of the black locomotive which was to pull our train to Cornwall. A kindly porter assisted us into the first-class carriage and walked with us along the narrow corridor to help us find our seats. I thanked him as he placed our luggage on the rack. The compartment was small but adequate, with red seats, numbered above.

I caught sight of my reflection in the mirror which was located under the luggage rack. I was aghast to see specks of black soot dotted on my face and when I looked at Molly could see she was speckled the same. I dabbed both our faces with my lace handkerchief.

'Oh, miss,' Molly squealed with obvious delight, 'this is the most wonderful thing that has ever happened to me. I can't wait to get going.'

I seated myself by the window as she spoke, wondering if it would be proper to remove my bonnet. Deciding to do so, I laid it on the seat beside me, with my reticule, and looked out of the window at the goings on.

Without any warning, the carriage jolted and we could hear the hissing of the mighty engine. At the same moment, a piercing whistle was blown and the train moved forward slowly with a chugging sound, gathering speed as we left the station.

'I feel quite elated,' I said to Molly. 'This is quite an adventure and I must confess I feel quite hungry.'

We both laughed as we partook of cook's luncheon which she had so kindly put together for us. As we ate, we looked out of the window and marvelled at the changing scenery. After the blacks and greys of the city, the countryside unfolded like a colourful ribbon speeding by.

We arrived at Penzance at four o'clock in the afternoon. Molly and I stood outside the station, our light luggage around our feet, scrutinising each carriage which arrived. Half an hour passed and I was feeling restless. Surely my grandmother hadn't forgotten our arrival time. I was just about to go and ask the stationmaster if there were any messages for Miss Merriock when a voice startled me.

'Jane Merriock?'

The voice was deep and questioning, and as I turned to face its owner, I was pleasantly surprised. The gentleman was tall and well-built with fair hair and deep brown eyes set in a handsome face. He was smart but his clothes rested on him casually, in fact his whole manner was of a casual nature. His eyes smiled into mine.

'Why, yes,' I stammered and felt foolish as I said it.

No-one had caused this effect on me before. He bowed almost mockingly before me.

'Robert Thornton at your service, Miss Merriock. Your carriage awaits.'

I followed him without question, Molly at my heels. The carriage was an open one and, Robert Thornton handed me a grey woven rug to cover my legs as the late September afternoon was chilly. Molly sat up front next to the driver, so I was left with this stranger for a companion, and an interesting companion as it turned out.

Robert Thornton sat opposite me on the plush seat, his eyes surveying me and, I thought, waiting for me to speak. I did, for the question had been hovering on my lips.

'And what rôle do you play at Pendenna Reach, Mr Thornton?' I asked him sweetly.

He looked at me a few seconds before replying.

'I'm your grandmother's estate manager, your grandfather's when he was alive, and have been for ten years. I trust that we will become good friends, Miss Merriock.'

It was a statement rather than a question. He leaned towards me and smiled, and I thought his hands were going to reach out for mine, but they relaxed in his lap. He looked at me seriously.

'You must feel strange coming to see a Grandmother you've never met.'

'You are right, Mr Thornton, it is a very strange feeling, but I know from my grandmother's letters she is as eager to see me as I am to see my late mother's home.'

There was something else I had to know.

'Can you tell me, Mr Thornton, who else lives at Pendenna Reach?'

'Your Aunt Laura.'

He leaned back. Did I sense contempt in his voice? My mother had spoken of her sister, Laura, who had been engaged to be married, but her betrothed, Andrew Trehaine, had disappeared mysteriously the same time as my mother left Pendenna.

'Is she married now?' I asked tentatively, wondering if had any cousins.

'No,' was all Robert Thornton replied and I sensed by his manner that was all he would say about Aunt Laura, for now at least.

I looked around at the countryside, thinking how different this land was to the hustle and bustle of London. Small, whitewashed cottages were dotted here and there amongst the fields and hedgerows. My companion pointed out various landmarks.

We neared the top of a hill and I could see the sea shimmering in the late afternoon sun, and on the cliff I caught my first glimpse of the house. Robert Thornton must have heard my sharp intake of breath, for the house was far larger than I'd imagined. It stood stark and grey against the backdrop of the blue sky. Then we dipped down over the hill and it vanished from view.

'You are impressed?' my companion queried with a smile.

'Why, yes,' I stammered. 'I had not imagined it to be so immense.'

As I spoke, we pulled up at the tall black wrought iron gates where we stopped momentarily for the lodge-keeper to open them. I felt the butterflies in my stomach and had not imagined that I would be so nervous. Robert Thornton then threw propriety to the wind and laid a hand over mine.

'Do not worry, Miss Merriock, you will be made welcome and will always be safe while I am here.'

Although taken aback by the touch of his strong hand, the unexpected encounter gave me courage and I felt quite bereft when he drew away.

As we rounded a bend I caught my first close look at the house. Sea mist had started to curl around the chimneys, but many of the mullioned windows still glinted in the late sun. Mr Thornton helped me alight. I felt weary and apprehensive as the great oak door swung open as if in greeting.

Molly disappeared with the carriage and I forced my aching limbs to move forward to the door. Then something suddenly troubled me.

Had I imagined Mr Thornton uttering the word safe?

2

The housekeeper, Mrs Dobbs, greeted us as we stepped into the vast hall. She was a small, plump woman, her grey curly hair escaping from a bun drawn back carelessly from her kindly face. She was dressed in black from head to foot, a large bunch of keys jangling at her waist. I quickly took in my surroundings, noticing a fire burning cheerily in the large, stone hearth. Mrs Dobbs saw me glance toward it.

'The house gets chilly this time of year in the evening, Miss Merriock, and we wished to give you a warm welcome. If you follow me, miss, I'll show you to your room.'

As I followed Mrs Dobbs, I glanced back at Robert who gave me an encouraging smile. I noted the huge portraits covering the stone walls and guessed them to be my ancestors. The red carpet beneath my feet had at one time been thick, but sadly was now almost threadbare in places. As we reached the top of the wide staircase, corridors stretched to the right and left, and were rambling, as my mother had said. Even now, oil lamps were lit to dispel the impending gloom of evening. I followed Mrs Dobbs. It seemed we passed a hundred doors before she opened an oak door on our right.

'This is the yellow room, Miss Merriock, your mother's until she left this house over twenty years ago. We hope you'll be very comfortable in here.'

I stepped into a room which gave the appearance of continual sunlight. The heavy curtains and bed hangings were of a yellow damask material. The heavy rug on the polished floor was interspersed with large yellow roses. Even the pictures were of all things yellow. I looked around me with delight.

'It is a beautiful room, Mrs Dobbs,

and even more so as it was my mother's.'

Mrs Dobbs stood in the doorway, a gentle smile on her face. I longed to ask her if she'd known my mother, but thought it best to wait.

'Your grandmother will be delighted you are so pleased. She is anxious to meet you.'

I was as anxious to meet her, and was a little disappointed that she had not greeted my arrival. At that moment a man appeared behind Mrs Dobbs.

'Miss Merriock's bags,' he said in a thick accent quite unfamiliar to me.

The housekeeper thanked Thomas, as he was called, and he carried my bags into the room.

'I will send your maid to you shortly. You are no doubt tired after your long journey and such a lot to take in.'

As she spoke she moved toward the door.

'I will tell the mistress you have arrived,' she added, and closed the door.

Like a child, I twirled around and

almost ran to the full-length window, eager to see the view. There was a balcony, I noticed, and excitedly I undid the window catch and stepped out on to it, leaning over the stone balustrade. I was at the front of the house, but I could see nothing, the mist was now so dense. I guessed the sea to be on my left as I could hear the muffled sound of the waves crashing on the rocks. I was disappointed but prayed for a clear day tomorrow.

I had the rest of the day to deal with first, and the thought of the meeting with my grandmother brought the butterflies back to my stomach. I had a fleeting thought of Robert Thornton, wishing he were near. As I fastened the catch on the window, there was a light knock at my door and Molly appeared. I could sense she was as excited as I was.

'Oh, miss, what a lovely room,' she enthused. 'I'm to share a room with Lizzie, as some rooms are being done up.'

'And is she nice, this Lizzie?' I asked, anxious to ascertain that Molly was content.

'Why, yes, miss, except she talks sort of foreign.'

At this I smiled, thinking of Tom.

'Miss, we must get you ready for dinner. We are to meet Mrs Dobbs at the head of the staircase at seven-thirty so you can meet your grandma.'

I quickly undid the ribbons and removed my bonnet while Molly lit the lamps. A maid brought water and filled the hipbath. She never spoke a word and just bobbed a curtsey as she left. I sank gratefully into the scented water and washed the grime of the day's journey away while Molly unpacked what little clothes I had with me. I would be glad when our possessions arrived by coach at Penzance the following day.

Molly helped me into my pale blue silk evening dress and redid my hair in the chignon I so loved. The finishing touch was the pearls my papa had given me on my sixteenth birthday. I looked at the finished result in the full-length mirror on the wardrobe door. My reflection pleased me.

All too soon it was nearing seven-thirty and we made our way to the staircase where the housekeeper was waiting. Molly left us and I descended the stairs with Mrs Dobbs, feeling quite confident, until I caught sight of Robert Thornton in the hall below. He was dressed for dinner in a black jacket and white shirt. My legs suddenly turned to jelly and I caught hold of the banister as he looked up at me, following my progress.

'Miss Merriock,' he murmured meeting me at the bottom of the staircase, 'I've come to wish you luck.'

He smiled and I suddenly felt confident again. As Mrs Dobbs led me to the door of the drawing-room, I took a deep breath before entering. I stepped into the huge drawing-room and quickly took in the tall french windows opposite with heavy blue velvet drapes.

Out of the corner of my eye I could see a fire burning merrily in the large stone fireplace.

'Thank you for coming, my child.'

I heard the voice before I saw my grandmother. There was a rustle of stiff taffeta and as the shadow moved towards me I could see she was dressed entirely in black with a lace mantilla over her greying hair. The only hint of colour came from a large emerald ring she wore on her left hand. Although Grandmother was in sombre dress, her person was anything but. I had imagined her to be tall and austere but the plump and pretty face looking at me was suffused with joy. Suddenly the cloud which hung over me disappeared for I knew that she was sincerely pleased to see me. She held out her hands to me.

'Jane, my dearest child.'

I almost ran to her, placing my hands in hers. Then she clasped me to her and I was engulfed in a soft, fragrant embrace. She held me at arm's length.

'How lovely you are, child, and so much like your mother. I believe you have her charm and will bewitch any young man who looks at you.'

'Oh, Grandmother!' I exclaimed huskily, scarcely able to believe my good fortune. 'I was so afraid you might not really want me here.'

'Not want you, my dear child? I have been counting the days.'

As she spoke, she indicated for me to be seated on the floral couch by the hearth. She seated herself opposite me and pulled the bell chord by her side. In what seemed no time at all, a maid appeared.

'Ah, Lizzie, please light the lamps and replenish the fire.'

My grandmother spoke softly, all the while surveying me by the firelight. Her next words addressed me.

'You are not spoken for?'

The question puzzled me.

'I have never met a gentleman who reached my expectations.'

As I spoke, I thought fleetingly of

Robert Thornton, so was amazed at Grandmother's next words.

'You have met Robert, my estate manager. I hold him in high regard. It would please me greatly if you and he could be good friends.'

There was no answer to this and I guessed Grandmother expected none as she continued.

'Tell me about your mother, my dear. Was she happy?'

'As happy as any person could be, with the man she loved. They've made me happy, too, and it was a great loss when they died.'

The thought of them saddened me. My grandmother must have sensed my mood for she laid a hand over mine.

'You have me now, my dear, and I have you. I have wanted to know you since your birth but your grandfather was very stubborn and ruled this house with an iron hand. Far too harsh he was at times, I felt, but when one is married to such a man . . . '

Her words trailed off and I understood. She wanted me to understand my mother's banishment was not of her making and I believed this to be so. My grandmother wanted me to talk of my mother as she continued.

'Do you have any possessions belonging to your mother, Jane?'

'A small chest holds her valued treasures but I have not been able to bring myself to open it.'

This was true. The thought of looking through my mother's things upset me and I had put it off many times, despite my curiosity. Grandmother's voice cut across my thoughts.

'Perhaps now you are in her home it will be easier for you, my child. Your mother kept a diary, you know, maybe more than one. She let no-one see them. It would be nice to think you will find them so that you will have some insight into her life here.'

We had no more time to talk as at that point Robert Thornton entered the room, accompanied by a pleasant-looking, dark-haired woman. As my grandmother rose, so did I to face the newcomer who appraised me with piercing, cold blue eyes and I instinctively knew I faced an enemy.

'This is your Aunt Laura, your mother's elder sister.'

There was no similarity between my mother and her sister, Laura. My mother had been fair and tall, Laura was short and dark.

She held out her hand condescendingly toward me and I took it with as little grace as she offered it. My spirits sank as Aunt Laura linked her arm almost intimately through Robert Thornton's. He had been watching the scene before him and suddenly spoke in a soft, authoritative voice.

'I shall escort Miss Merriock into dinner as she is our guest,' he said, much to my aunt's displeasure.

Dinner was a quiet affair, interspersed with trivial conversation. We sat at one end of a vast table in a huge dining-room with red walls, which by the end of the meal started to swim before my eyes. I excused myself as I was obviously over tired and the soft bed in my room beckoned me.

As soon as I stepped into my room, I knew someone had entered it while I was at dinner. A trace of perfume, not my own, lingered in the air. I looked around but nothing seemed to have been disturbed. Then I saw it — a piece of grey paper on my dressing-table. I stood transfixed for a moment before picking it up in my trembling hand. The words leaped up at me.

LEAVE PENDENNA BEFORE IT IS TOO LATE.

Who would write such a thing? I screwed the paper up fiercely and threw it in the wastebin. As I climbed into bed, I wondered if I had a friend or an enemy at Pendenna and guessed it to be the latter.

3

Although tired, I slept fitfully that night. The unfamiliar bed plus creaks and groans from the house contributed to my sleeping and waking. I imagined the mist whispering conspiratorially through the cracks in the old, stone walls. I must have fallen into a more restful slumber in the early hours as I awoke with a start to the sound of Molly drawing back the heavy curtains. She turned and saw I was awake.

'It is a glorious morning, miss. Did you sleep well? You look a little dark under the eyes but perhaps this will refresh you.'

She placed a tray laden with tea and bacon with scrambled eggs on the bed. I hadn't realised how hungry I was after picking at my dinner the previous evening. I ate and drank while Molly tidied my clothes and tipped steaming water out of a huge pitcher into a china washbowl. I idly wondered how on earth she had carried the water up the stairs.

On climbing out of bed, I went to the window and stepped on to the balcony, eager to see the view. All the mist had vanished and I could see the sun glimmering on the calm sea. I realised the house was built on the edge of a precipitous cliff and tried to imagine a path to the sea below. Suddenly I was eager to explore my surroundings just as I heard Molly tell me to get back in before I caught a chill and realised I was in my nightshift.

'Lawks, miss,' Molly said, fussing around, 'you will catch your death.'

'Don't fuss so, Molly,' I admonished lightly as she helped me into an emerald green day dress. 'I am anxious to explore and I would like you to come with me, Molly. My grandmother doesn't rise until late and I promised to meet her for luncheon. Aunt Laura takes breakfast in her room.'

'And rarely leaves it,' Molly cut in, 'or so cook says.'

I turned at Molly's words.

'But I met her last evening. She was quite sociable, if somewhat aloof.'

'Sorry, miss, it's not for me to say.'

'Don't worry, Molly. I want you to tell me everything about the people in this house even if it is idle kitchen gossip. Come, we have a lot to do before luncheon. I will take my cream shawl because the morning air could be chill. Run and get yours and I will meet you in the hallway.'

'But, miss, I ain't allowed out the front way, Cook says.'

'When you are with me you can go out any way. Now run along.'

While waiting for Molly in the hall I remembered Robert Thornton mentioning the stables to the rear of the house. That would be my first place to visit. While not an accomplished horsewoman, I had learned to ride in Paris and enjoyed it.

The sun shone warmly from a clear

blue sky as Molly and I made our way to the rear of the house. We lingered to look out to sea as Molly had never been out of London till yesterday. She didn't, however, seem overawed by the scenery before us.

'It's not as wild as I thought it would be,' she observed.

'Not at this moment, Molly, it is true but the sea has many moods and this is only one of them. I know it can be very wild.'

I ventured toward the cliff edge much to Molly's dismay as she stayed rooted to the spot. As I got nearer, peering over the cliff, I could see that below lay a small cove covered in shingle and rocks. I could see a path zig-zagging down towards it and couldn't wait to get down there but guessed Molly would not be keen to accompany me. No matter, I would find a moment to go myself. I stepped back and made my way to Molly who was relieved to have me back safely by her side.

To the rear of the house was a

full-length courtyard and we could see the stables at the far end. As we approached, I could see a female mounted on a grey horse and as we neared I could see it was Aunt Laura. Her horse was restless and I wondered why she waited.

'Good morning, Aunt,' I ventured pleasantly. 'What a beautiful mount.'

'This is my mare, Misty. Did you sleep well, Jane?' she enquired and I thought how different her manner was this morning and wondered if I had imagined her hostility the previous evening.

Before I had time to reply, Robert Thornton appeared, leading a large black horse, a magnificent-looking creature.

'Do you ride, Miss Merriock?' he enquired graciously.

'Indeed I do,' I replied with pleasure.

'Then tomorrow perhaps you would care to accompany your aunt and myself. We could ride to see the Dancing Damsels, an intriguing stone circle a short way from here.'

'I would be pleased to if my aunt is willing.'

I looked at Aunt Laura. Did I imagine the hostility return to her eyes?

'I will be glad to ride with you, Jane. You could take Amber, a gentle mount. On my return I will arrange for her to be saddled tomorrow.'

My aunt's reply could not have been more courteous.

'That is settled then. Come, Thunder,' Robert Thornton said as he swung himself into the saddle. 'I will see you at dinner, Miss Merriock.'

Molly and I found a pleasant rose garden to the side of the house where we sat for some time enjoying the warmth of the sun amidst a fading riot of colour. How lovely this must look in the height of summer, I mused. On glancing at my fob watch, I realised with dismay it was nearly time to meet my grandmother. Molly made her way to the side entrance while I crossed to the front of the house. Glancing up, I noted where my room was. It was easy to pick out as it had the only balcony. I was about to look away when a movement at the window caught my attention and I was astonished to see a woman's face looking down at me, watching me. I turned away and looked back. I had not imagined it — it was still there.

I picked up my skirts and ran to the door. Swiftly I ran up the staircase and along the corridor, intent on finding who would be so presumptuous as to enter my room, but on reaching it and flinging wide the door, the room was empty. All that remained was the lingering scent of lavender I had detected the previous evening.

As I pondered over this little mystery, a ray of sun glinted through the window casting its light on the rug beneath my feet. It was then I noticed my luggage, my mother's polished chest included, stacked neatly against the wall. Perhaps it had been a maidservant looking down on me, but I dismissed the idea.

Whoever it was was the same person who had left the note while I was at dinner the previous evening, I was sure of it.

Looking at my watch, I realised I was late. I glanced at my reflection in the mirror, smoothed my hair and removed my shawl. As I reached the foot of the staircase, Mrs Dobbs crossed the hall from the direction of the drawing-room. She stopped and smiled her cheery smile when she saw me.

'Miss Jane, your grandmother is waiting for you on the terrace where luncheon has been served as it is just the two of you. Are you settling in? Is there anything you need? You only have to ask, you know.'

With that, she paused.

'I'm fine, thank you, Mrs Dobbs. I noticed my luggage has arrived.'

'Yes, miss. Thomas took it up. I let him in your room as it arrived just after you went out this morning.'

So there had been no maidservant in my room. The whole incident puzzled me and as I made my way through the drawing-room, I had every intention of asking my grandmother who it could have been.

The tall french windows were open and led out on to a delightful terrace. Grandmother was sat at the end of a table laid with cold meat and salad. She smiled when she saw me.

'My dear child, come and sit by me.'

She patted the cushion on a wicker chair next to her.

'Tell me what you've been doing this morning.'

'I'm so sorry to be late, but the time went so quickly,' I apologised.

'Apology accepted, Jane. Tea, my dear?' she asked and as she poured from a while china pot she continued. 'I know how it was when I came here as a bride nearly forty-five years ago, so much to see both inside and out. I spent days exploring, as I am sure you will do.'

'Why, yes, Grandmother, I am impatient to see the rest of the house and the beautiful cove I glimpsed this morning,' I replied enthusiastically. 'Is it all right for me to wander through the house?' I asked eagerly.

'Of course it is, child. I want you to think of this house as your home and if you have any questions, Mrs Dobbs will be only too pleased to help. Of course, the rooms in the east wing are no longer lived in. It is where the nursery and the schoolroom are but since your mother and Aunt Laura grew up, no children . . . '

Her voice trailed off. I looked up at her and saw a woman saddened by her memories. It may not have been the right time to ask about the occupants of the house but nonetheless I had to know.

'Does anyone else live here with you, Grandmother, other than Aunt Laura and Mr Thornton?'

Did I imagine the hesitation before she replied?

'Why no, dear, apart from the servants, of course.'

She changed the subject quite quickly and was smiling once more.

'Now tell me, Jane, do you read?'

'I most certainly do, Grandmother.'

'It would please me so much if you would read to me sometimes, dear. My eyesight isn't what it once was and the library is at your disposal. One other thing, Jane, your Aunt Laura. If she seems unfriendly at times, take no heed. She has never got over her betrothed, Andrew Trehaine, disappearing before their marriage.'

We spent the next couple of hours talking, mainly of my mother. I learned more of her childhood and I in turn told Grandmother of my childhood and Mother's life in London. Not once was my father mentioned but given time I felt sure he would be.

We left each other about four o'clock so my grandmother could have a rest before dinner. I returned to my room. On entering it I could see instantly that my belongings had been put away. Molly had obviously been busy while I was downstairs. Mother's chest stood against the wall. Now was as good a time as any to open it. I retrieved the key to unlock it from my trinket box and as the lock clicked back I opened the lid slowly, almost reverently. I suspected that the chest held the fabric of my mother's life. I kneeled on the floor, surveying the contents which lay before me, still laid neatly in order despite the moves the chest had been through.

On the top lay a long yellowing envelope. I took it in my hands and stared down at it. The words *Marriage Certificate* were written on the front in my mother's neat, bold handwriting. I sat on the armchair by the window and took the certificate slowly out of the envelope. Unfolding it, I could see my mother's name, Felicity Ann Pendenna, and my Father's, John Merriock. It was the date that jumped up at me — November, 14, 1852. I worked it out quickly in my head and realised my mother had been four months pregnant with me when they had married.

4

I was still turning over in my mind my parents' wedding date the next morning while Molly helped me into my riding habit. If Grandfather had known about my mother's pregnancy I could see why he would be incensed but to have let the ill-feeling last until the day he died, that, I could not understand.

Looking out of the window, I observed small waves chasing each other to the shore and the sun shining on the water sparkled like precious gems. I thought of my mother and how she would have looked down on a scene such as this all those years ago.

'You are thoughtful today, miss.'

I turned as Molly spoke.

'I've been thinking of my mother.'

I glanced at the chest against the wall. What other secrets did it hold, if any, I wondered.

'She was a good person, miss, and always kind to me.'

How true this statement of Molly's was. No matter that Mother had left this house in some disgrace, she was good and kind. This thought cheered me and I realised how much I was looking forward to my ride. On reaching the stables, I found Aunt Laura already sat on Misty while the stablehand held Thunder's reins. Robert Thornton held those of a delightful light brown mare with a golden patch over one eye.

'Oh, she's beautiful!' I said as I walked quickly towards where she stood.

Robert Thornton handed me a lump of sugar and as I offered it to Amber she took it from my hand, nuzzling her wet nose against me.

'There you are, friends with her already, Miss Merriock,' Robert observed as he swung up on Thunder while the stable-hand helped me mount.

All the while, Aunt Laura watched

and never spoke a word so I thanked her for Amber which she acknowledged with a nod of her head. Bad manners was the thought that crossed my mind but with Aunt Laura living in the countryside all her life perhaps drawing-room etiquette had eluded her, although I tended to think her bad manners arose from my intrusion on her and Robert Thornton's time together.

As we rode along the side of the house, Robert Thornton stopped and I slowed down beside him.

'Have you noticed the small fishing village of Polgent, Miss Merriock?'

As I looked in the distance to where he had indicated, I could indeed see a small harbour with some craft moored.

'How delightful. Maybe we could go there one day,' I suggested, but it was Aunt Laura who answered.

'That is one place I won't be accompanying you to.'

As she spoke she turned to the front of the house. Robert Thornton and I had no option but to follow her, leaving me quite perplexed.

'Mr Thornton, may I ask about the small cove below the cliff?'

'You mean Pendenna Cove?'

'Oh, it belongs to the house? Is it private then?'

'Indeed it is, Miss Merriock, and if you have intentions of going down there may I suggest you take good care? The path is steep.'

This I had already realised, but made a mental note of Robert Thornton's words of warning.

Our horses trotted along at a leisurely pace, with Aunt Laura a short way ahead of us. I had thought to take the opportunity to converse with her this morning but she obviously felt in no mood to do this as I chatted idly to Robert instead all the while thinking how regal he looked astride Thunder. The horse and his master appeared to tower over Amber and myself. Every now and then I patted Amber's head and whispered soothingly in her ear, wishing to gain her confidence.

We passed several cottages dotted here and there amongst the hedgerows. One in particular caught my eye. It had an old, thatched roof with white-washed walls, and a short path with fading flowers either side led to the black oak door. Without consciously realising it I had reined Amber to a halt.

'I don't know if I should be the one to tell you this,' Robert Thornton's voice came drifting to me.

'Tell me what?'

'Your namesake lives there.'

I turned back to look at the cottage again and as I looked, the door opened and an elderly woman with white wispy hair bent and placed a bucket by the door. As she stood up she smoothed her hands across the front of her white apron. She gave us only a cursory glance before going back inside.

'My namesake?' I asked somewhat stupidly.

'Yes,' Robert Thornton said, looking down at me. 'That was old Granny Merriock.'

My mind was working overtime as he led me onward. She had to be a relative, family of my father. I had every intention of returning to the cottage and knocking on the door, maybe with Molly, for in view of Robert's words I was sure it was some sort of secret. I had no desire to mention it to my grandmother before I had spoken to this Granny Merriock myself.

As we reached our destination, I caught a glimpse of the church with its squat tower reaching above the trees in the distance. When I took notice of where we were I had a sudden intake of breath. Before me in the field was a circle of weathered stones, each some five foot high. Robert Thornton had dismounted, but Aunt Laura had decided to stay on her horse. She had obviously been here many times before.

'Miss Merriock, may I help you down?'

Before I could answer, his strong hands had encircled my waist as he swung me to the ground. His hands lingered for a matter of seconds and I felt the colour rise to my cheeks. Why did this man have such an effect on me? Aware of his gaze and the knowledge he had noticed my confusion, I turned my face away from Aunt Laura who was watching us intently with, I felt, veiled emotion. As Robert let me go I realised Aunt Laura's affections lay in his direction and began to wonder if mine did also.

I moved around the stone circle, counting as I went. There were thirteen stones, each the same height, a few inches shorter than myself but not as tall as Robert. There was something earthy and evil about them and I felt half-afraid and half-drawn to their overbearing dominance. I had certainly never seen anything like it before, nor had I felt the presence of something so evil. It was almost tangible. I moved away, wanting to get back to Amber and home to Pendenna. Robert caught my arm gently.

'You are surely not afraid, Miss Merriock?'

'No,' I lied. 'What is the legend you mentioned?'

'On the Sabbath, the damsels were dancing although forbidden, so they were turned to stone.'

'And do you believe this, Mr Thornton?'

'We all believe what we want to believe, my dear, but do not be afraid of anything, especially while I am near.'

I thought of his words as we rode back to Pendenna and recalled with some pleasure him calling me dear and I no longer felt afraid.

Mrs Dobbs met me in the hall with a silver salver which she held out to me. I picked up the small cream-coloured card. On reading it, I realised it was a calling card from a Jason Trehaine.

Thanking Mrs Dobbs and clutching the card in my hand I quickly made my way to my room. I knew from experience living at Amy's that it was usually some time before a stranger in the district received a calling card. To have received one so soon meant there was a good reason. I suspected that Jason Trehaine was in some way related to Aunt Laura's betrothed. It was too much of a coincidence for him not to be, but even so what could he possibly want with me?

Looking at the card again on reaching my room, I realised Jason Trehaine had indeed invited me to call at Mannamead, his house in Polgent, at three o'clock on Tuesday afternoon. I recalled that Polgent was the small fishing village Robert Thornton had pointed out to me that morning and where Aunt Laura had said she would not go. I partly understood the reason now. A visit to Polgent would have brought back painful memories of Andrew Trehaine.

So I would take Molly with me and realised I would need some conveyance. I would have to seek out Robert and ask if he could arrange it for me. I was not altogether sure if Grandmother knew of Jason Trehaine's visit. Mrs Dobbs had told me my grandmother was indisposed and would see me at dinner. Could it be Jason Trehaine's visit had upset her?

While eating luncheon alone on the terrace I set to wondering where Aunt Laura and Robert ate their lunch and thought that perhaps they ate together. This conclusion on my part did nothing to ease my already overactive mind. Many questions were whirling around in my head. Who was the face at my window and who had left the message on the scrap of paper in my room? Why was Aunt Laura so hostile towards me when she knew nothing about me? And now why would Jason Trehaine, a man I didn't know and who didn't know me, invite me to his home?

As I had been left to my own devices that afternoon, I decided that it being such a glorious afternoon, I would explore Pendenna Cove. I calculated that the tide would have gone out by now so it was as good a time as any and I wanted to be alone with my thoughts. The hall was empty as I passed through and let myself out. I took a quick look back before stepping out down the steps and into the sunlight. I had the strangest feeling that I had escaped, but from what? Certainly not my grand-mother who had made me so welcome and it wasn't just Aunt Laura.

As I made my way along the cliff path and looked back at Pendenna Reach, I realised that the house itself was oppressive, maybe because of its age or had I become fanciful since entering its doors? I had not noticed the tall, soot-blackened chimneys before which reached upward towards the blue sky. I tried to shake off my morbid thoughts and concluded that I had not been the same since visiting the Dancing Dam-sels and vowed I would not go there again.

I had reached the top of the path which led to the cove below. It was indeed steep but to my relief a small handrail had at some time been constructed. Picking up my skirts, and holding on to the railing, I started the walk downward. I was overjoyed to see wild flowers growing in abundance on the cliff.

My mood had lightened and I suddenly had a spring in my step as I neared the cove below. Stepping on to the shingle beach, I stood for a moment and breathed in the salty sea air, walking precariously as the shingle was uneven in places. I headed for the sand the receding tide had uncovered, eventually sitting on a rock. I was alone with only the seagulls for company. Daringly, I removed my boots and stockings, enjoying the feel of the cold, damp sand beneath my feet. The warm sea breeze caressed my face and gently lifted tendrils of my hair. I felt more relaxed than I had since leaving London. Looking to my right I could see craft in the harbour, the glint of the sun catching the masts.

So engrossed was I with my surroundings and thoughts it wasn't until the last minute that I heard the crunch of shingle. As I whirled around, I saw, striding towards me, was Robert, his haired ruffled by the breeze. He was almost beside me and in my confusion I glanced down at my bare feet and gathered my boots and stockings in one hand.

'Janie.'

No sweeter word could have escaped his lips and tears pricked my eyes as the memory of my father uttering the same word sprang instantly to mind. I looked at Robert and, sensing my distress, his hands gently touched the top of my arms.

'I've upset you,' he whispered. 'For what reason I cannot imagine. Did I startle you?'

'No, it's just that you brought to mind the memory of my father who always called me Janie.'

The desire was so strong to touch his cheek I had to turn away.

'Apologies, Janie. I would not intentionally cause you distress. I don't know what makes me call you such. All I know is it seems the most natural thing to do.'

'There is no need for apologies, sir. It was just a sweet reminder.'

I turned back to face him, my hands still clutching my boots and stockings. As I glanced down so did he and we both laughed. The poignant moment was gone.

'You caught me unawares, sir, most unladylike.'

'No, it is good that you sense the beauty of nature. I caught sight of you and wished to warn you that the mist will roll in suddenly.'

Even as Robert spoke, I could see a haze starting to form on the horizon.

'And, Janie, if I may call you by your name, please address me as Robert. Let us be formal no longer.'

Sitting back on the rock, I proceeded, as discreetly as I could, to put my stockings back on. I noted that Robert averted his eyes until my stockings and boots were in place once more. I stood up, adjusting my skirts, at the same time looking at Robert's broad back and thinking all the while how dependable he seemed. Gently I touched his arm and he turned to face me.

'I shall call you Robert from this moment.'

His answer was to smile.

'And as you say, we should get back to Pendenna before the mist overtakes us. I remember on my arrival mist shrouded the house.'

We headed back across the shingle and to me it seemed the most natural thing to do, walking alongside this man who was barely a stranger. My heart leaped at his nearness and I prayed silently that he felt the same.

5

I awoke next morning after a restless night dreaming that I walked down the aisle with a faceless bridegroom by my side. These fanciful thoughts must stop, I chided myself, and the thought of the day brought me back to reality. It was today I was to meet Jason Trehaine.

After dressing, I intended to look through Mamma's chest, but I stood looking out of the window for some time. Grey clouds scudded across the sky where there had been none the previous day. The sea looked a murky colour and not at all as inviting as the day before. For some reason, since yesterday, I had taken some aversion to the house and wondered idly what a winter spent here would be like.

Grandmother had already said how nice it would be to have me here at Christmas time and I could not disappoint her but at this moment Amy's comfortable drawing-room and cheery nature seemed far more inviting, but now there was Robert. The thought of being far from him filled me with such sadness. My heart was here and I knew this was where I should stay.

Lifting the lid of Mamma's chest, I immediately set eyes on her marriage certificate but today I dismissed this intending to find out the truth at some later time. I lifted out four dark red books embossed with gold filigree and on each bottom right hand corner were the initials F.A.P. printed in gold. I opened the cover of one, and printed on the fly-leaf in my mother's hand was written, **The Diary of Felicity Anne Pendenna, July 1850**.

Skimming quickly through the pages I could see it was a daily account of Mamma's life here at Pendenna, and one name jumped out at me from the page — Jason Trehaine. I read the paragraph.

August 15, 1850.
Today Laura and I walked to the church with Andrew and Jason Trehaine. Laura has eyes for Andrew who is tall and dark, Jason on the other hand is fair and not a lot taller than myself. We hope to walk with them again on Sunday afternoon.

My mouth formed a smile as I thought of my mother at the age of sixteen. It is always hard to imagine one's parents at that age. I looked forward to reading these diaries on a dreary day but I had spied something else in the chest. A small blue velvet box was tucked away in the corner where it had lain beneath the diaries. I picked it up and instinctively knew that whatever this box held was going to have a marked effect on my life, or so I thought. On opening it, I could see it contained a small brooch Mamma had worn for as long as I could remember. It was so familiar to me but as it lay in the palm of my hand it was as if I had never seen it before.

A heart-shaped pale violet amethyst was set in gold which surrounded the stone and was fashioned in small hearts. It looked very dainty but was in fact quite heavy. I turned the brooch over and could see some letters inscribed on the gold backing. Peering closely at it in the light from the window I made out the words, *I adore you for ever.*

I stood for some moments thinking of the words and how romantic they were and yet I had never thought of my father as a romantic. How wrong one can be! Deciding to wear the brooch that afternoon, I placed it back in its velvet box on my dressing table. It would go well with my lilac-coloured dress which I intended to wear to make as good an impression on Jason Trehaine as I could. Jack, the head stablehand, was to convey Molly and myself to Polgent. I guess Molly was pleased about this and was sure she had a soft spot for him as she had mentioned him on a couple of occasions.

Placing a heavy shawl around my shoulders, I made my way outside. On passing through the hall I collided with Robert as he walked from the library.

'Robert, I'm so sorry. I was daydreaming as usual.'

'My dear young lady, it is I who should be apologising. I was in far too much of a hurry. Forgive me.'

He looked at me, smiling, and I was jelly under his gaze.

'Where are you off to, Janie? It is today you are visiting Mannamead, of course.'

It was a statement rather than a question.

'Why, yes,' I stammered, 'though why Mr Trehaine would request my company, I do not know.'

'He's a good man, Janie. I know him well. I'm sure that he is anxious to meet Mrs Pendenna's granddaughter after all this time. He and Andrew were good friends of your mother's.'

'So Andrew is Aunt Laura's betrothed, Mr Trehaine's brother?'

'Indeed he is, or was. We will talk some other time of the Trehaines but for now would you please excuse me, Janie? I shall be late for an appointment.'

So saying, he cupped my face gently in his hands and kissed me on the forehead. Almost before I had time to realise what had happened Robert was gone.

As I made my way to the rear of the house with the intention of exploring the small, wooded area behind the stables, I pondered over the kiss that Robert had placed on my forehead, but my sensible side told me to dismiss it. However, my heart sang with the thought that Robert held some affection for me.

On the edge of the wood, I hesitated. Even in the light of day, it appeared dark and forbidding. The large oak trees were set quite far apart but the boughs of them overlapped one another, shutting out the sky above. Boldly I stepped on to the moss-covered ground, twigs snapping gently beneath me here and there. The farther in I went, the darker it seemed, then I stopped in my tracks for I fancied I could hear voices.

Straining my ears, my heart pounding in the stillness, I realised it wasn't a fancy. Someone was indeed speaking, not far from me. I moved as quietly as I could behind a large tree trunk in the direction of the sound, picking my skirts up so they would not disturb anything. Peering around the gnarled tree trunk I clamped my hand to my mouth so as not to let my gasp of surprise escape my lips.

Robert and Aunt Laura were stood together in a small clearing, his hands holding her arms as he had held mine and they were gazing at each other. Their words I could not hear, just the murmur of their voices as they spoke softly to one another. Tears sprang to my eyes and, picking up my skirts, I ran back out of the wood.

As I reached the edge of the wood

and ran across the gravel, I heard Robert's voice calling my name. I ran on, my breath coming in short gasps as I raced through the house, past a bewildered Mrs Dobbs. On reaching my room, I shut the door and stood with my back to it, sobs escaping me as I thought what a fool I was to even think that such a man as Robert Thornton could fall in love with me.

An hour later, I had composed myself and had decided resolutely to treat Mr Thornton with the contempt he deserved. There was a sudden knock at the door and my grandmother entered, leaning heavily on a silver stick. My heart sank as she surveyed me for some moments before she spoke softly to me.

'What is wrong, Jane? Mrs Dobbs tells me you rushed past her not an hour since as if you had the devil at your heels.'

I turned away from her gaze, not wishing to be rude but also not wishing to tell her the truth.

'It was a large bumble-bee, Grand-mother.'

As I faced her, the small lie just escaped my lips.

'And would you cry over a mere bumble-bee, Jane? I think not, for you have been crying, and don't deny it. I may be getting old but I can still see when a young woman has been reduced to tears.'

I faced her stubbornly, not wishing to change my story.

'Please sit down, Grandmother,' I said and I led her to the armchair by the fireplace. 'Bumble-bees do indeed fill me with dread and I was afraid of being stung as I was when a child. My tears were tears of relief that I had not been.'

Grandmother continued to look me up and down. Her eyes were keen and I knew she was taking in my dishevelled appearance and red eyes.

'We will speak no more of it, but needless to say I do not believe you. I had hoped you could confide in me as your mother used to but I see you do not wish to speak the truth. However, I do believe a person of the male variety is involved and that you have been sorely disillusioned. As there is only one man it could be, I can guess, but not why. Perhaps sometime in the near future you will tell me, for now I suggest you send for Molly, dress for your outing and join me for lunch before you go.'

She had a very authoritative voice and I felt very meek on the receiving end of it as I pulled the bell. I assisted Grandmother to her feet and walked with her to the door. Before she left she turned and said to me, 'Please convey my kind regards to Mr Trehaine.'

Two hours later, attired in my lilac-coloured day dress which was adorned with cream lace on the v-neck bodice and long sleeves, my matching bonnet and cream lace gloves and my mother's amethyst brooch firmly in place, I stepped into the open carriage with a composure I did not entirely feel. Molly tucked a travelling blanket across my lap and joined Jack up front for our short journey to Polgent. I really was apprehensive, as on other occasions in London I had always been accompanied by Amy.

The scenery looked completely different on such a grey day compared to when Aunt Laura, Robert and I had ridden on horseback to see the Dancing Damsels, but the grey sky matched my sombre mood. I knew Molly had been aware that something was amiss but as always she kept silent.

As we passed Granny Merriock's pretty cottage, I resolved to visit her on the morrow. It wasn't far to walk and I prayed silently that the weather would be kind. My spirits had lifted suddenly and I pushed Robert to the back of my mind and set to wondering about Jason Trehaine. I was curious to know what Mannamead was like and wondering what sort of man Mr Trehaine would be.

It wasn't long before we were turning

into a short, hedge-lined drive. The house was enchanting, Georgian in style and white walled, with an aura of wealth. The tall windows were grey today but I could imagine how, with the sun shining on them, they would sparkle.

Jack helped me down from the carriage and while he and Molly rode around to the servants' quarters, no doubt for a cup of tea and cake, I smoothed my skirts, pulled the shawl farther around my shoulders and walked up the many steps to the front door and pulled the bell. It was several seconds before an elderly manservant opened the door to greet me, revealing a beautiful hallway with a green and white mosaic floor. Relieving me of my bonnet, shawl and gloves, Simms, as he told me he was called, went off in the direction of one of the many double doors, leaving me to take in my surroundings.

The hall was light and spacious and my eyes were drawn to the ornate ceiling above me. There were two alcoves either side of the tall, marble fireplace, in each standing a partly-clothed stone statuette. Intricate pillars embraced each double door and a stone balcony ran around each side of the hall, reached by an intricate staircase. I could see the upper door quite clearly. Compared to the clean shabbiness of Pendenna Reach, this was opulent and yet it appeared hardly lived in. Plush rugs in bright colours of red, gold and green were placed outside each door and in front of the fireplace there were two high-backed chairs with red and gold braid.

A portrait under a light caught my eye. It was of a very handsome young woman with dark, curling hair and bright blue eyes. Although handsome, she looked delicate. Her face looked down on me and no matter where I stood, the melancholy eyes followed me. She wore a white organza dress with a high bodice and short, puffed sleeves. The white rose in her hair accentuated the black of it. Curious to know who she was I moved nearer to look at the writing on the small plaque beneath.

'It is my wife, Charlotte,' a man's gentle voice cut through my thoughts. 'She died of consumption two years after we married.'

How long he had been there I could only guess, but turning to look at the owner of the voice I could see he was a man of about forty-five years with light hair greying at the temple. He was taller than I and slender of build but there was something familiar about him and I wondered idly if we had met before. He came towards me and held both hands out which I took in my own, instantly liking this man.

'Jane Merriock, welcome to Mannamead. I am so delighted to meet you. I knew your mother well when she was a young woman. I felt such sadness when I knew of her passing.'

Momentarily, the smile vanished from his face.

'Mr Trehaine, I am pleased to be here and to make acquaintance with one of my mother's friends. Although she never spoke of you, I have heard of your friendship.'

His smile returned and he led me into the drawing-room. It was as grand as the hall and I looked about me in awe. The ornate fireplace dominated the room with a carved surround. A large, brass fender surrounded it with a cheery fire burning in the grate.

'Apologies for my rudeness in surveying the room, Mr Trehaine, but you have a beautiful home.'

'Even more beautiful if I had someone to share it with, but after . . . I never loved again.'

He paused, then smiled.

'Forgive me. Please be seated and I will ring for tea.'

I sat on a plush settee covered in green damask, and curtains to match hung at the tall windows. I realised how silly I had been to be apprehensive about visiting Mr Trehaine but I now sensed a similar nervousness in him and deduced from what he had said that he wasn't used to female company. He rang a bell at the side of the fireplace and then seated himself opposite me.

'You're as lovely as Felicity, if you don't mind my saying so.'

His eyes regarded me with a warmth I could almost feel.

'Thank you, I am indeed like my mother and hope that my personality matches hers also, for she was gentle and kind.'

I noticed the sombre expression had returned to his face, so to change the subject I glanced to the other side of the room. It was then I noticed, with startled surprise, several of my father's landscape paintings on the wall and I got to my feet and walked over to them, Mr Trehaine following me.

'These are my father's work,' I said softly, turning to him for some explanation.

'Indeed they are, Miss Merriock,' he replied and moved to the window. 'John was a good friend of mine and I bought them from him over a period of time, a long while ago.'

Accepting this without any question I carried on looking at the pictures before me. A tear fell down my cheek as I saw the embankment and the house where I spent so many happy years, painted by my father's hand. At this moment the door opened and Simms entered with a young maid who deposited a large tray on the table before the fire. This interruption pleased me as I didn't want Mr Trehaine to see me upset. We both took our seats again. I poured tea from a silver pot into delicate rose-coloured cups and we drank and ate small sandwiches while generally talking of Polgent and Pendenna and my childhood in London which we kept coming back to at Mr Trehaine's direction of conversation.

'And are you happy at Pendenna, Miss Merriock?'

The question was unexpected and I hesitated. Should I tell this stranger, who didn't seem like a stranger, my true feelings? I felt I should.

'Not completely is the true answer. My grandmother has welcomed me admirably but Aunt Laura is very cool and indeed almost rude. I find the house oppressive. Your home is more favourable.'

There, I had said it, actually spoken the words as to how I had felt since entering Pendenna Reach. Jason Trehaine had listened without interruption. He placed his cup on its saucer, looking at me thoughtfully.

'Aunt Laura is a very unhappy woman and has been since my brother, Andrew, disappeared a week before they were due to marry. This doesn't excuse her manner towards you but may contribute towards it. The house itself is, as you say, oppressive, due to its dark rooms and almost granite-like exterior so I do understand how you feel.'

'And there is a smell of lavender often in my room, which mystifies me.'

'This I cannot comment on, but appraising you, I am certain you are a sensible young woman and not prone to flights of fancy, so the fact that you do smell lavender I do not dispute. There is probably a simple explanation.'

I really enjoyed my afternoon at Mannamead and felt quite sad when I left. Just before I seated myself in the carriage, Mr Trehaine took my arm and spoke softly to me.

'You will be welcome to stay here at Mannamead any time you may choose, Miss Merriock. Please don't forget that.'

I left with these words ringing in my ears and thought with some pleasure how I would look forward to our next meeting.

6

Molly helped me dress for dinner that evening. I picked the prettiest dress from my wardrobe hoping to impress Robert Thornton. It was made of silk and the turquoise colour shimmered in the evening light as Molly helped me into it. I decided not to adorn myself with jewellery of any type but leave the creamy whiteness of my throat bare.

Adeptly, Molly fashioned my hair up in a soft style and covered it with a delicate lace snood which matched the colour of my dress. I looked at my full-length image in the mirror and moved sideways so I could admire the silk train. I was more than pleased with my appearance.

'You look beautiful, miss,' Molly enthused. 'The colour suits you perfectly.'

'Thank you, Molly. Don't ask me

why but I wish to look my best this evening. Now run along for your meeting with Jack.'

We both grinned at one another for Molly had confided in me of her proposed meeting with Jack that evening. How I wished I could confide in Molly, but to tell the secret of one's heart to a servant, even one as dear as mine, just wasn't done. Making my way downstairs, I glanced at the grandfather clock in the hall and realised with some misgiving that I was a trifle late. Standing outside the drawing-room door, my hand on the doorknob, I took a deep breath before I entered. As I opened the door and stepped into the room I could see they were all assembled, plus a young man who was a stranger to me. They all looked up at me as I stood there and Robert was the one to break the awkward moment.

'I will get you a drink, Miss Merriock,' he said going to the drink trolley, and I was grateful to him even though I was still smarting at his betrayal that very morning.

Grandmother, dressed entirely in black from head to foot, beckoned me to sit by her on the settle by the fire, a seat I had on previous occasions found most uncomfortable. I seated myself and took a small glass of sherry from Robert with a demure thank you, hardly able to look him in the eye for fear of him reading my thoughts.

Aunt Laura was dressed in a yellow gown which did everything to enhance her dark colouring. Even as I looked, she caught hold of Robert's arm and I was angry with myself at the pang of jealousy which shot through me. I realised this gesture was deliberate on her part as she looked straight at me with animosity, a secret little smile hovering on her lips.

The newcomer had been in earnest conversation with Robert until he had been interrupted by my aunt. He was not as tall as Robert but he was dark and prepossessing. Grandmother's voice cut into my reverie.

'How did your meeting with Mr Trehaine fair today, Jane?'

'Why, very well, thank you. Mr Trehaine is a charming, friendly man. I like him very much and Mannamead is quite lovely,' I enthused, smiling at my grandmother.

'I'm pleased you liked him, Jane, for he was a good friend of your mother's. How I wish things could've been different.'

Her words trailed off and a faraway look had replaced the inquisitive one.

'In what way?' I asked, for it seemed my grandmother had made some sort of implication concerning my mother and Jason Trehaine.

'No matter, Jane! It is an old woman's rambling,' she said and abruptly changed the subject. 'Robert please introduce my granddaughter to our guest.'

Robert Thornton headed towards us with the stranger at his side. I stood to be introduced. Maddeningly the colour rising in my cheeks at Robert's nearness.

'Miss Jane Merriock, this is Alan Lester, my good friend who is a historian at Cambridge.'

I proffered my hand which Mr Lester took gently in his own.

'It is a pleasure, Miss Merriock. Robert has told me much about you.'

Had he indeed, I smarted, and gave Robert a look of dismay which was returned by a mocking smile to which I was becoming most accustomed. Indignation flowed through me at the casual way he looked at me as if nothing had happened earlier that day. At this point, we were interrupted by Mrs Dobbs to say that dinner was ready to be served for which I was thankful.

The table was laid as I had not seen it before, silver knives, spoons and forks of the best quality, white serviettes in silver holders and goblets rimmed with gold. At the centre of the table was a beautiful flower arrangement of yellow roses in a silver bowl. I guessed this was in honour of our guest, Alan Lester. I was thankful I had taken such trouble earlier when I dressed for dinner. Grandmother took her seat at the head of the table and startled us all when she spoke.

'Please be seated by Robert this evening, Jane.'

As she sat down, Robert held the elaborate dining chair for her. I saw Aunt Laura glance in my direction, a scowl on her face as she seated herself by Mr Lester. So it was, I sat close to Robert at the dinner table with our guest opposite me, much to Aunt Laura's distaste. While eating our first course, I addressed Alan Lester to break the uncomfortable silence.

'You are quite far from home, Mr Lester. Are you on holiday or is it some other reason which brings you to Cornwall?'

I smiled at him and realised all at the table were waiting for his answer.

'To tell you the truth, Miss Merriock, I am here to study the stone circles in this county,' he said quietly as if only to me, but it is indeed like being on holiday. I understand from Robert that you visited the Dancing Damsels.'

'Why, yes, only last week.'

'And what was your opinion of this piece of history?'

'I found it fascinating, but also decidedly evil.'

'I had no idea you felt this way, Miss Merriock,' Robert's voice drifted across to me. 'Did you, Laura?'

'I agree with Jane.'

My aunt, who rarely spoke in my presence, surprised me at her words.

'It is no matter to me whether I see them again or not for the whole place fills me with dread.'

'My dear ladies, you have nothing to fear. Is it mere superstition which makes you think thus?'

Alan Lester sat back in his chair. His voice had become stronger and I realised he thought passionately about this subject.

'It is not only superstition, Mr Lester, but an enormous, tangible feeling of menace.'

Aunt Laura obviously felt very strongly about this.

'You have no need to fear folklore. Believe me when I say this for the stone circles are in fact attributed to the Druids and are certainly not maidens turned to stone. I assure you that history is fascinating and not to be feared. We have history all around us. Why . . . '

He paused, his hand indicating our surroundings.

'This house is a prime example. I wouldn't doubt there is a priest's hole somewhere in this building. Would you fear that also?'

I glanced across at Aunt Laura and saw her face had paled significantly and her hand was clenching the serviette she held, her knuckles turning white.

'There is much talk of it,' my grandmother now joined the conversation, 'but one has never been found.'

She turned to Laura.

'You were fascinated by this when a young girl, weren't you, Laura?'

'Yes, Mother. Both Felicity and I searched the house from top to bottom,' she said, her voice trembling as she spoke, 'but we found nothing. So, Mr Lester, this assumption is unfounded.'

'Yet I would have bet my life on it, but I bow to your knowledge of the house, Miss Pendenna.'

Mr Lester bowed his head briefly in my aunt's direction.

'We will change the subject now,' my grandmother interposed. 'Let us talk of lighter things, like my charming granddaughter, Jane, who has brought such light into my life.'

Grandmother raised her glass of wine as she spoke.

'To Jane. Long may she stay at Pendenna Reach and come to love it as all Pendennas before her.'

I felt weak with embarrassment as I watched them all raise their glasses, Aunt Laura reluctantly, Alan Lester with a guest's enthusiasm and Robert, well, he looked toward me glass in hand, and said quietly, 'To Jane.'

After a delightful evening of witty conversation with Mr Lester, we stood in the hallway to bid him good-night.

On reaching me he whispered, 'Hold fast when you have it.'

I looked at the others but thankfully no-one had heard him. As I looked into his dark sparkling eyes I realised the words had indeed been meant for my ears alone. What had Robert been telling this man? I felt my cheeks go hot once more as I saw Robert looking at me, that secret smile on his lips once again.

No sooner had I climbed into bed and nestled into the feather mattress than a thunderstorm started to rumble in the distance. It wasn't long before it had moved nearer. I got out of bed and, drawing back the curtains, stood silhouetted as I watched the lightning dance across the water. The thunder appeared to shake the foundations of the house as each clap got louder and even nearer.

The storm made me restless and I knew there would be no chance of sleep so, putting on my robe, I made my way to the library with the intention of selecting a novel. As I stepped into the corridor, the house seemed even more eerie at night. Candles still flickered in the sconces and the dim light cast my shadows across the walls as I moved slowly towards the staircase. Before descending, I glanced almost furtively around me. The clock startled me as it chimed the hour of three. The sound of it appeared louder at night and I marvelled that I could not hear it in my room, the walls being so thick.

On opening the library door, I was even more startled. Robert was sitting in an armchair, a book open on his lap. He was just as surprised to see me but quickly gained his composure.

'Are you frightened of the storm, Jane?'

As he spoke, I was very aware of my attire. I pulled the open robe around me and bunched my loose hair over my shoulders.

'No, sir, I am not afraid but restless and thought to find a book to read.'

'Come and sit by me and let us engage in some conversation while the storm rides itself out. I feel like some companionship and yours would be most welcome.'

As he spoke, Robert indicated the empty armchair opposite him. As I hesitated in the doorway, unsure as to whether to go backward or forward, Robert got to his feet and walked towards me, his hands outstretched. In that moment my resolve to be aloof to him dissolved and, trembling, placed a hand in his and let him lead me to the armchair. As I sat down, Robert placed a finger very gently on my bottom lip, bending to me, his eyes looking into mine.

'Has anyone ever told you, Janie, that you have the prettiest mouth?' he whispered.

I was lost for words and was sure his intention was to kiss me but he moved to the fireplace to replenish the fire.

After stirring the pine logs he leaned his hands toward the blazing warmth while I watched the flames that leaped in unison towards the chimney, lighting the room with a golden glow. The only other light was from a lamp on a small table.

'There are plenty of books,' Robert said as he moved away from the fire his arm indicating the book-lined walls, 'but it would be difficult in this light to choose. Maybe you could peruse the shelves later, in the light of day.'

'Indeed,' I agreed.

I made to get up off the chair but Robert stopped me gently with one hand and sat leaning forward in his chair, his hands clasped casually in front of him. The light from the fire outlined his good looks and I could see the fire reflected in his eyes. I suddenly realised I was staring at him and averted my gaze.

'Don't look away, Janie. I sensed at dinner you were displeased with me.'

It was a question and brought to

mind his association with Aunt Laura and my anger returned for I would not and could not share him with another woman. What had happened to me? Never before had I responded to a man with such feelings.

'I would very much like to know what you said about me to your friend Alan Lester.'

'Only the truth.'

'Which is?'

'That you are a beautiful, young woman and that I hold you in high regard, but there is something else bothering your pretty little head and I can guess what.'

'If you know, why ask? It should be I asking the questions.'

'A woman's body, a child's mind,' he whispered.

His words cut deeply. I knew it was true. I was behaving like a sixteen-year-old and it wasn't the impression I meant to convey to this man.

'I apologise for behaving as such,' I said meekly, 'but soon after dropping a kiss on my brow, I see you in intimate conversation with Aunt Laura.'

I could've eaten my words for they conveyed the truth, that I was indeed jealous. I saw the startled smile on Robert's lips and then it vanished.

'Don't press me on this, Jane. Believe me when I say the meeting with your aunt was purely innocent.'

He looked more serious than I had seen him before and I half believed him.

'Let us talk no more of it.'

I knew for the moment at least, the subject of Aunt Laura was closed.

'Tell me, Jane, have you any aspirations?'

The subject was indeed changed. Should I tell him my one aspiration was for him to fall in love with me? But, no, I thought of my days prior to coming to Pendenna Reach.

'I don't know that it is an aspiration, more a desire to travel, to see places I have only read about. The Leaning Tower of Pisa at dawn, following the footsteps of the Egyptians, walking through the sand on a foreign shore or seeing the moon glimmer on the Serpentine. It is but a dream.'

I looked at Robert who was watching me attentively.

'How did I know you would be different from most young ladies of your position? The majority would aspire to find a husband and raise a family.'

He watched my face as he spoke. How I wished to kiss his strong mouth.

'Dreams can come true, Janie. Would you wish to share this world adventure with someone?'

The question came quite unexpectedly and I wished with all my heart to answer it adequately. I cast my eyes on the dying embers in the grate and then looked back at Robert.

'Only with someone who truly loved me, and loved me enough to share my dreams.'

There was a pause for what seemed like a lifetime yet it was only seconds.

Robert bent forward and cupped my face in his hands and gently brushed my lips with his. I wished that moment could have lasted for an eternity but it was gone and I felt a trembling through my whole body and was afraid when I got up that my legs would not hold me. The clock in the hall struck the hour of five, each chime seeming to move us further from that precious moment.

'I must go,' I said and realised my voice did not sound the same.

Nothing would be the same again.

'Yes,' Robert's voice came to me as if in a mist. 'The maid will be in soon to lay the fire.'

So saying, he rose to his feet and helped me to mine. As I walked to the door, I heard him call my name softly.

I turned to look at him, my hand on the doorknob.

'Trust me,' he said.

As I opened the door, I knew that a girl had entered two hours before and a woman was leaving, a woman very much in love.

7

I made my way back to my room along the now dark corridor as if in a daze. As I shut my bedroom door behind me, I leaned back on it, savouring again the moment Robert's lips had briefly touched my own. What joy filled my whole being at the memory then I recalled his words, trust me, and I really believed that I did with all my heart.

It was still dark and, suddenly feeling cold, I lit the lamp on the small table by my chair and bent down to light the fire laid ready in the hearth. As I sat watching the paper alight and listening to the dry crackling as the flame caught the wood, I thought of my mother and how she must have come back to this very room with a heart full of love and longing for my father. The thought of her brought to mind her diaries. This was as good a time as any to read some more.

Swiftly I retrieved the second diary from the chest for I was anxious to know at which moment she had fallen in love. As I skimmed through the pages, the entries were of mundane things, such as visits to a dressmaker, church outings and my mother's and Aunt Laura's walks with Andrew and Jason. From what I read, I gathered Mamma and her sister were very close. Then I sat upright in my chair as I read an entry near the end of the diary.

October, 12, 1851.
Today Laura and I discovered the priest's hole quite by chance whilst dusting the doll's house. It was amazing, but Laura has sworn me to secrecy, why I can't imagine. I am longing to tell Mamma but will not for I do not want to be the recipient of Laura's bad temper. I just hope Miss Blackstone does not find out as

she has eyes which are sharp and a tongue to match.

The words jumped up at me and I thought with some dismay of Aunt Laura lying and denying any knowledge of the priest's hole to Alan Lester only last evening. The question was, should I keep it a secret also or should I tell Grandmother? I would mull it over in my mind and decide what to do. There was no more mention of the priest's hole so quickly I replaced the diary in the chest and reached for the third one with some excitement. As I leafed through the pages I realised this was more revealing and was what I was seeking.

March 1, 1852, I read.
Oh, what a day. My heart is singing for he kissed me. My first kiss! I swear I am in love and can hardly wait to see him again, to talk and laugh with him and maybe feel his arms around me.

April 5, 1852.
Laura is jealous that I am in love and that I don't spend much time with her, but she and Andrew appear to be getting along well. I earnestly hope she will find the happiness I feel for I am deliriously happy. My every waking moment and my dreams are filled with thoughts of him.

June 4, 1852.
If this is love, what joy. I am suffused with such fulfilment I pray that it will last for ever.

June 28, 1852.
Laura told me she and Andrew were walking out together. She mentioned the priest's hole today and hoped I hadn't told anyone. In all honesty, I had forgotten about it. Laura also said I seemed different, not at all the Felicity she knew.

July 18, 1852.
Two things of importance happened

today. Laura announced she is to marry Andrew Trehaine in November. She doesn't act like a woman in love. Today I realised that I was with child! What are we to do? My beloved will know.

October 20, 1852.
Papa refuses to let me marry and says I have brought nothing but shame on the Pendenna name. I have confided in Mama. She understands but cannot go against Papa. What he says is final. Tonight I shall cry myself to sleep, if sleep will come, for my mind is in turmoil. Laura has no sympathy for the position I find myself in. It is as if she hates me.

This was the last entry in the diary and to my surprise there was only one entry in the fourth diary.

November 7, 1852.
Today we are to leave for France. Granny Merriock came to the house

today and told me not to have anything more to do with her grandson but John is noble. My heart is filled with sadness for I will be leaving all that is familiar to me and what is worse, I cannot say goodbye to dearest Mama but I have to be strong for the child I carry. All I can wish for is that Papa will change his mind when the child is born. Farewell.

Tears sprang to my eyes as I imagined my mother's pain and at that moment I hated the Grandfather I had never known and Granny Merriock, being no more understanding it appeared. What my parents must have gone through for me. Tears rolled down my cheeks as I replenished the fire, leaned back in my chair and drifted into a troubled sleep.

Molly startled me into wakefulness gently shaking my shoulder.

'Why, miss, what is wrong? Are you ill? And the curtains all drawn back, and it's hot in here.'

Molly's anxious face looked down at me and I remembered, as if in a dream, the night's events and I felt emotions both happy and sad.

'It's all right, Molly. It was the storm that kept me awake,' I assured her as I bent down to pick up Mama's diary which had slipped to the floor.

As I got up to place it in the chest, I could see that the rain was pouring down which would prevent me from my much-desired visit to Granny Merriock, but no matter. I had the desire to get ever closer to my mother and would visit the schoolroom instead. Suddenly I remembered Molly's meeting the previous evening with Jack. So bound up was I in my own thoughts I had forgotten Molly and I realised she did seem especially happy this morning. On asking her how she faired, Molly replied with a sparkle in her eye.

'It was really good, miss. Jack is a real gentleman, and, miss . . . '

'Yes, Molly, go on.'

'He kissed me.'

Her voice trembled as she spoke and it brought to mind the early hours of the morning in the library and although she would never know it, I knew exactly how she felt and thought how strange it was that we should have gone through the same experience on the same night.

I had hoped with intense longing that I would see Robert that morning but alas there was no sign of him. I would have to wait. I ate breakfast in solitary silence, alone with my thoughts. As I then made my way across the hall to the stairs, Mrs Dobbs crossed from the kitchen towards the library.

As she passed me, she asked, 'Did the storm disturb you, miss?'

She looked at me almost knowingly and I suddenly felt guilty. As I made my way to the schoolroom, following Mrs Dobbs' directions, I told myself not to be fanciful.

As I opened the door of the room, the first thing to catch my eye was a doll's cot! It looked totally out of place amongst the desks, blackboard and easel. As I walked over to the wooden crib, I could see there was a large, porcelain doll in it, tucked up with blankets and wearing a white lacy bonnet. How strange, I thought.

'I wonder what you are doing in here,' I said aloud.

The four wooden desks were badly ink marked, the white china inkwells caked in ink. I lifted the lid of each desk and in the last one there was a notepad on which had been written in large capital letters, **I HATE YOU**. It has obviously been written with some feeling as the pencil had pressed hard on to the paper, piercing it in places.

Who would have written it and about whom? It was hard to tell if it was done years ago or quite recently. As I walked across the wooden floor to the blackboard, my boots sounded very loud. I started to write the name **Felicity** with the white chalk I found when I detected the smell of lavender. Turning swiftly, I came face to face with the lady who wore it.

The tall, grey-haired, gaunt-looking woman who stood in the doorway was dressed in clothes of a past age. Her hair was parted in the middle, the side hair being drawn over the front of her ears and then looped up to a small bun at the back of her head. She wore a dark blue dress with black stripes, printed at the waist, the full skirt falling gently around her, and on her head a white day-cap trimmed over the ears. She just stood there and looked at me. I felt somewhat ill-at-ease and sensed she was waiting for me to speak first.

'Who are you?' I uttered softly.

There was a pause before she spoke, in a Welsh accent.

'I know who you are. You're my Felicity's little one. I watched you arrive from this very window and have watched you on many occasions since.'

As she spoke, she took a couple of steps into the room, her skirts swishing on the wooden floor and the waft of lavender became more apparent.

'You are correct,' I said, 'but it doesn't tell me who you are and why you had the right to enter my room without invitation, for it was you, wasn't it, and you left me the warning note?'

My voice was unsteady and I spoke with an authority I didn't feel.

'Yes, it was me who entered your room, but only because of my concern for your safety.'

'It pleases me that you admit it but I must ask you again, who are you?'

As I spoke, she moved farther towards me and picked up the china doll, gently smoothing the doll's dress. I noticed her eyes were a fading green as she looked directly at me.

'I am your mother's governess, Nora Blackstone. Felicity was a good girl, so gentle and kind, to animals as well as people. I am still waiting for her return. The nursery is in readiness.'

She paused and laid the doll back in the crib.

'But don't you know?' I said gently. 'My mother died some years since.'

'No-o-o-o.'

The word became such a wail it frightened me but then she calmed down.

'Felicity will return to me. She promised and Miss Felicity never breaks a promise. Laura on the other hand, she is cruel and unfeeling with a harsh streak in her, like her father, Morgan Pendenna.'

She grasped me by the shoulders so suddenly I trembled.

'It is because of Laura you must leave. She will do you harm and I want no harm to come to my Felicity's girl.'

'But why? Why would she harm me? She is my mother's sister.'

Her hands relaxed their hold on my shoulders for which I was glad and I moved away from her and sat on the chair by the ink-stained desk, my knees trembling.

'I cannot tell you why. You will learn soon enough. If you will not go then I must protect you some other way. Miss Laura only comes to see me to make sure I'll keep my mouth shut.'

She suddenly clamped her hand over her mouth and I could see tears rolling down her cheeks.

'You see, Jane, it is the priest's hole. No, I cannot and will not speak of it for fear of my life.'

'Tell me, Miss Blackstone, what is it you fear so much? I may be able to help you. I will speak to my grandmother on your behalf.'

I felt sorry for her now. She was obviously a very frightened woman.

'I cannot tell you. Just believe me when I say there is such horror to be found in these walls and to think it is the nursery where my beloved Felicity lay so sweetly as a child, sleeping like a baby. That is how I shall see her again one day when she returns and all will be well again.'

I knew now there was something very odd about Miss Blackstone's ramblings and tended to think I should not believe a word she told me for it was quite plain to me that she was living in the past.

'Where is your room, Miss Blackstone?' I ventured.

'Why, next to the nursery, of course, where it has always been. Don't you remember?'

She spoke to me as if I was a child.

'Come with me, Felicity, back to the nursery, like a good girl. Lessons are over for today. We will get our coats and walk in the wood like we used to. Come, child.'

She held out her hand toward me.

'I cannot come now, Miss Blackstone. I have to see my grandmother.'

I waited with baited breath but she seemed to accept this.

'Later then, child. I am feeling weary now.'

So saying, she looked at her fob-watch.

'Polly will be bringing my lunch any time now and then I will make sure everything is ready in the nursery.'

'Miss Blackstone,' I had to ask, 'why is the crib and china doll in the schoolroom?'

'Why, don't you know? I couldn't let Felicity's baby lie in the nursery, poor little lamb. She will be safer here.'

Thankfully, she walked to the door then and paused and looked back.

I knew she was back in the present when she said quietly, 'Watch out for Laura, child, but I will protect you if needs be.'

She then left the schoolroom and I could hear her skirts swishing along the corridor. To say I was confused about this meeting was very true. I was left baffled by the conversation I had just had with my mamma's former governess. Was there really a priest's hole or was it something conjured up by a woman not of sound mind? And while Aunt Laura had not been as affable as I would have liked, was she really so evil?

As I made my way down the stairs, along the dimly-lit corridors, determined to find Grandmother, I felt a panic rising in me and longed to escape to normality, but where? My thoughts turned to Jason Trehaine. How I wished I were at Mannamead now, in the light, airy rooms. Instead I was here, stifled by the suffocating atmosphere of Pendenna Reach. I wondered now, although no harm had yet befallen me, if I would be safe in my bed.

8

My grandmother wasn't to be found in the drawing-room and looking out of the window I could see the rain still fell relentlessly and guessed she would not be out on the terrace either. I would seek out Mrs Dobbs, hoping she may know her whereabouts for I was anxious to talk to her about many things, Nora Blackstone being number one on my list.

Not since arriving at Pendenna had I entered the kitchen, Mrs Dobbs' domain. I tentatively pushed open the door and was faced by an alarmed-looking, buxom woman dressed in black with a frilly white apron and mobcap. Stood beside her, up to her elbows in flour, was an equally-alarmed-looking girl, as slight as cook was buxom, tendrils of hair escaping her white cap.

'Can I help you, miss?' Cook asked, her rolling-pin suspended in mid-air.

As she spoke, the young girl drew one arm across her forehead leaving a smudge of white flour down one side of her plain face.

'Agnes, how many times have I told you not to do that? Now run off and wash your hands and face.'

So saying, Cook gave her a little push with the rolling-pin and Agnes scuttled off.

'Sorry, miss, this is what I have to put up with. Now, what can I do for you? A nice cup of tea, perhaps? I take it you are the mistress' granddaughter, Miss Jane?'

She paused for breath and I spoke quickly.

'Yes, I am indeed Jane Merriock. I'm sorry to intrude but was wondering if you could tell me where I may find Mrs Dobbs, please.'

Cook had gone back to rolling her pastry. She stopped long enough to indicate with her rolling-pin a door to her left. As I stepped into the large kitchen I took in the huge black range over which hung pots and pans of various shapes and sizes. The wooden table on which Cook was baking was immense and took up a third of the kitchen. Various dishes were scattered on the top of it and flour was everywhere. As I stood taking in my surroundings, Agnes returned looking much tidier and ready to immerse her arms once more into the large mixing bowl.

'I'm Nelly, miss,' Cook said, stopping her rolling-pin once more in mid-air. 'It's pleased we are to have you here. Your mother was very much loved by all. I won't say more, miss, it's not my place, except to say as how I don't agree with what happened. Would've given me notice in but I loves the mistress and nothing will change that.'

I was lost for words but as Nelly resumed her rolling I uttered, 'Thank you, Nelly, I understand.'

I walked to the door she had

indicated, and stepped into a small corridor. I guessed it was the door opposite me which I needed for the one on the right was marked pantry. I knocked gently on the door and Mrs Dobbs' voice called, 'Who is it?'

Opening the door a fraction, I saw Mrs Dobbs get up from her chair and smooth her skirts.

'Oh, it's you, miss, come in, please.'

The room was small but comfortable and very warm. I felt quite stifled and was pleased when Mrs Dobbs asked if I would partake of a glass of lemonade. Seating myself on a high chair stood against the wall, I looked around me at the many ornaments placed on small tables scattered around the room. There was hardly a space left on the walls as they were covered in pictures, mainly of the sea and coastline. On a table beneath the window were small, stuffed animals which I found quite distasteful and looked quickly away at the small fire burning in the grate, listening to the rain as it splattered against the window pane.

I gratefully accepted the glass Mrs Dobbs gave to me and sipping the cool drink slowly I asked her where I could find my grandmother. As I spoke, a bell tinkled above my head. Looking up I could see three rows of bells, thirty-six in all, which I hadn't observed before.

'That's the mistress now, miss. She is still in bed as she suffered one of her bad heads today and has taken a powder. She will be wanting a cup of tea, so if you would like to come with me, miss.'

'Will that be all right?' I asked between gulps of lemonade.

'Of course, my dear. The mistress will be pleased to see you.'

I was glad to escape the stuffy atmosphere as I watched Mrs Dobbs place a guard in front of her small fire. In no time at all, Nelly had prepared a tray of tea for two and sandwiches and I found myself following Mrs Dobbs up the now-familiar staircase. Instead of turning right as I did to my room, we turned left and stopped outside the third door on the right. Mrs Dobbs tapped lightly on the door and entered, balancing the tray on one hand.

'You have a visitor, madam.'

I followed Mrs Dobbs into the room and could see my grandmother sat up amongst many pillows in a huge, carved, four-poster bed which dominated the room. She was dressed in a white cotton nightdress, a white lace bed jacket covered her shoulders and arms. Her grey wavy hair fell loose around her shoulders and it was covered in a white lace cap. It seemed strange not to see her in black, and propped up against the white pillows she looked almost ethereal.

'Why, Jane, what a delightful surprise. Come and sit by me.'

I moved across the carpet to sit on the chair at her bedside. Before seating myself I placed a kiss on her cheek.

'I hope this isn't an imposition, Grandmother, but I wish to talk with you.'

'It is not an imposition and tell me, child, what is it you wish to talk about?'

I glanced at Mrs Dobbs who was busy placing a tray in front of my grandmother.

'Pay no heed to Daisy,' Grandmother coaxed. 'There is nothing that can't be said in front of my housekeeper after forty years of loyal service. Come, Jane, what troubles you, for you do look troubled? Pour the tea, please, Daisy.'

Grandmother was looking at me in anticipation of my words.

'Well,' I began, 'I'd like to know more about Nora Blackstone.'

Both women looked at each other and then at me. The cup and saucer Daisy Dobbs held was suspended in mid-air. There was a pregnant pause before my grandmother spoke at last.

'I take it you have met Miss Blackstone,' she said quietly, 'and where was this, pray tell me?'

'In the schoolroom, not an hour since.'

'And what were you doing in the

schoolroom, Jane?'

I was afraid she was going to avoid the issue of Miss Blackstone.

'I wanted to see where Mama spent her childhood and in view of the weather, I thought today a good time to explore the house. Miss Blackstone came upon me as I wrote on the blackboard. I smelled the lavender and was intrigued, as she had on occasions been in my room. The scent was the reason I knew it was her.'

'And what did you make of our governess, Jane?'

'Very strange in manner and very obviously living in the past.'

At this point I wondered if I should mention the priest's hole but decided against it for some reason.

'You are right, Jane. Nora Blackstone is indeed odd.'

Grandmother took a sip of her tea.

'This is why we allowed her to stay here for she would never have gained another position and I felt sorry for her. I still do for she never steps outside these walls. What she finds to do with her days I cannot imagine. Laura visits her from time to time, I believe, but to gain any information from my daughter is like getting blood from a stone.'

She paused and I noticed her cheeks had become very pink and her eyes bright.

'Will that be all, madam?'

Mrs Dobbs spoke as if to break a spell and my grandmother just waved her hand in dismissal. Mrs Dobbs looked at me and I was sure she was going to say something, but she opened the door and shut it almost silently behind her.

'Are you all right, Grandmother?' I asked anxiously as her whole manner had changed. 'Please have a sandwich and sip your tea. I'm sorry if I have upset you in any way.'

She laid her hand on mine.

'Please do not distress yourself, dear. You haven't upset me but, Jane, please don't believe anything Miss Blackstone says. She is muddled in the head and has been since your mother left. For some reason, she cannot bring herself into the present. If you see her again, don't take anything she says seriously. Now tell me, how are you getting on with Robert?'

I got used to my grandmother changing the topic of conversation but this question brought Robert to my mind and I could feel the colour suffuse my cheeks and I felt transparent under my grandmother's close scrutiny.

To prove the fact she said, 'Ah, Jane, I see you have succumbed to Robert's charm. Not surprising, and to say I am pleased is barely sufficient. I must be honest and say I have high hopes of a match of my lovely granddaughter and Mr Thornton. He is a good match for you, Jane, and you for him as you have spirit, the Pendenna spirit.'

I just sat and listened nonplussed at her words and when I left her some time later I was walking on air to think my grandmother would give her blessing to a match between Robert and myself. My heart sang with joy.

★　★　★

Three weeks passed without incident since that eventful day when Robert kissed me and I had met Nora Blackstone. October turned to November, the trees laid bare, their branches and the sky and sea merged into one, a dull uninteresting grey. Gone was the sun sparkling on the blue sea and in place of small waves chasing each other to shore the sea now crashed on to the shingle.

I'd seen Robert most days but never alone. I'd noticed that gone was the mocking smile and in its place had appeared an almost gentle, disarming one which melted my heart. It was Sunday and I awoke to the sound of Molly drawing back the curtains to reveal a watery sun and I realised that the incessant rain of the past weeks had at last stopped.

'Good morning, miss,' Molly said in her cheery voice. 'Looks like being a nice day, sun and all.'

As she spoke, she placed a lump or two of coal on the fire which was already burning in the grate. How cheerful it all looked. It was then I decided to accompany Grandmother to church. To Molly's amazement I got quickly out of bed.

'You haven't had your breakfast, miss.'

'Leave it on the table, please, Molly, and I shall sit by the fire to eat it. What is the time?'

I glanced at the small, tortoiseshell clock on the mantle.

'Nine o'clock! I shall have to be swift as I intend to go to church.'

'Right, miss, I shall lay out your clothes if you tell me what you'd like to wear.'

I got to my feet and looked through my wardrobe.

'I think the royal blue skirt and jacket with the fur trim.'

It was wool and I knew it would keep me warm. For prudence sake I would wear my black bonnet and gloves which were trimmed with blue to match my outfit.

I sat back at the table and poured myself a cup of strong tea and buttered toast. It had always been a ritual for Molly to bring me breakfast on a Sunday unless Grandmother requested my presence in the dining-room.

'Miss?' Molly's eager voice cut into my thoughts. 'I've got something to tell you, miss, which is really important and I can contain myself no longer.'

'Why, Molly,' I began and turned to look at her smiling face. 'Please, do tell me.'

'It's Jack, miss. He says he wants us to get wed and I am so happy to but won't give him an answer until I have your blessing.'

Molly looked at me expectantly and I stood and gathered her in my arms. I could sense the joy she felt and tried to feel how I would react if Robert asked me to marry him. I looked down at her as I released her, smiling at her obvious happiness.

'Molly, did you doubt that you would have my blessing? I am overjoyed for you and Jack. You must give him your answer today.'

Had I lost her, I wondered. Dear Molly, who had been the biggest part of my life since Mamma and Papa had died. As if in answer to my silent question Molly took my hand.

'I won't leave you, miss, but I cannot go back to London.'

She looked at me now, anxiety on her pretty face.

'I have grown to love it here, miss, and if Jack and I are blessed with children, the countryside is so much nicer than the city to bring them up.'

'Don't fret, Molly, I understand fully, and anyway I may stay at Pendenna myself. London does not hold much appeal for me anymore except, of course, for dear Amy. I just want you to be happy, Molly, and whatever happens we must not lose touch.'

'Never, miss, I promise. Now I must help you, for it is nine-fifteen and I believe Mrs Pendenna usually leaves for church at ten, or so my Jack has told me.'

It was a rush but at five minutes to ten, I was stood in the hall attired in my Sunday best, waiting for my grand-mother. I knew she would be pleased, as on other occasions I declined to accompany her on a Sunday to Pendenna church, but she had never pressed me. To go on my own volition was good. Since Mamma's and Papa's funeral, I had not stepped through a church gate. As I stood with my thoughts Mrs Dobbs interrupted them.

'There is a letter for you, Miss Jane. It is on the silver plate behind you.'

I looked behind me and picked up the letter she'd mentioned. It was from Amy. I tucked it safely into my black beaded reticule, thanking Mrs Dobbs just as my grandmother reached the bottom of the staircase with Aunt Laura by her side.

'My dear Jane, how lovely. I assume you are accompanying us?'

As she spoke, she linked her arm through Aunt Laura's just as Robert made an appearance.

'Please take Jane's arm, Robert. We must step into the carriage, for time is pressing.'

So, as the huge doors of Pendenna Reach opened, admitting an icy blast of wind, I found myself being escorted by Robert into the carriage. Aunt Laura sat in silence as she watched Robert and me intently. I glanced at her from time to time, idly taking in the smoothness of her skin and the beige-coloured outfit she wore. On glancing now and then at my grand-mother, dressed entirely in black, as usual, I could see her smiling indul-gently at us and now and then, she made some observation of the country-side while I kept casting my mind back to Molly.

Until today, I had only seen the church from a distance through the treetops. As we drew up to the lychgate and we stepped out of the carriage,

Robert's hand gently squeezing mine, I could see close up that the tower was tall and very obviously fifteenth-century, but the main body of the church was more recent. I had studied English churches and always felt it was such a pity that I never entered them anymore. Robert took my arm and we walked through the gate up the stone path, strewn with leaves. I listened to the monotonous sound of the bell ringing and tried hard not to look at the many dank grey gravestones which stood upright all around me.

We seated ourselves in a cold pew at the side of the church, very obviously reserved for the Pendenna family. As I cast my eyes over the congregation, it was then I spotted Granny Merriock. She sat near the front of the church not far from me. As I watched her she suddenly glanced in my direction and gave me such a venomous look, I shook and quickly averted by gaze.

The service over and back outside once more, shaking hands with a very tall vicar, I caught sight of Granny Merriock out of the corner of my eye as she walked to the gate.

'Excuse me,' I said to a startled vicar, interrupting him mid-sentence as I scurried off after her.

As I reached the gate an arm suddenly caught mine.

'Where are you going in such a hurry, Jane?'

I looked back to see Aunt Laura almost towering over me. Until now I had not noticed how tall she was.

'I just want a word with Granny Merriock, if you'll excuse me.'

So saying, I freed my arm from her grasp.

'I'll come with you, Jane, for this I must see.'

She then hurried after me, past the carriage, in the direction of the village but it was to no avail. There was no sight of the old woman. I stood looking around me with exasperation, Aunt Laura at my side.

'What a pity,' she offered with

obvious sarcasm in her voice.

'I would have caught up with her if you had not detained me, and what did you mean when you said, this I must see? What sort of spectacle were you expecting?'

As I spoke I hastened back to the carriage, Aunt Laura keeping up beside me.

'I was curious to see what reception you would receive.'

'By that, I assume you expect it to be unfavourable.'

We had reached the carriage and I turned to face my aunt.

'Why, yes, Jane, it is what I'd expect under the circumstances.'

'And what do you mean by that?'

My voice was becoming louder but I could not help myself.

'Why do you dislike me so much?'

'Whatever gives you that idea, Jane?'

'Because of your whole manner towards me. How could I have ever done anything to you for you to treat me with such disdain?'

'You are your mother's daughter.'

She almost spat the words at me and I was taken aback.

'Ladies, ladies!' Robert's voice interrupted us as Grandmother spoke up.

'Jane, Laura, please settle yourselves in the carriage. You are behaving like a couple of fishwives. I am most displeased and what Reverend Tomlinson thought of your rudeness, Jane, I can only imagine. What you have to quarrel about I don't pretend to understand. Now let us get home and thank goodness only Robert and I had to witness such behaviour.'

I felt quite humbled as Grandmother admonished us and caught the merest of smiles hovering on my aunt's lips and wondered what secret thoughts she had to smile about. Robert's face was expressionless and I prayed silently my behaviour had not spoiled our friendship.

On arriving back at Pendenna, Grandmother said she wished to speak with me before luncheon in her room.

Aunt Laura was to accompany her now. As I watched them climb the stairs, I wondered at my aunt's animosity towards me. I had thought my mother and Aunt Laura to be close.

'What was that all about, Janie?'

Hearing Robert's voice beside me, I realised that for once I had forgotten his presence.

'It was to do with Granny Merriock. Laura seems to think I will not be received well by her but tomorrow I intend to find out as I will visit her cottage and get to the bottom of this.'

'Then I will accompany you, Jane, and that is an order,' saying which he placed a finger gently on my lips preventing a reply.

Who was I to argue with this man? I felt sure his only desire was to protect me, but from what?

9

On reaching my room, I remembered Amy's letter and retrieving it from my reticule, sat by the window to read it feeling quite homesick.

My dear Jane, I read.
How pleased I was to hear all your news at last. I had quite expected to hear from you earlier but guess you and Molly are quite settled in Cornwall even though it must be a completely different way of life to that which you experienced here. I am still never without company or some ball or theatre to attend. I still miss you greatly, dear Jane, and am very afraid now that you may not return to live with me at Grosvenor Square. I do not say this to distress you but I want you to know that I understand for it is wonderful you

have at last met with family of your own. Think of me as a selfish woman who loves you but I am prepared to relinquish you, my dear, as long as you are happy.

After all the gallant young men I introduced you to here in London, each one of whom you didn't find the least bit interesting, I now find you have met your match and have lost your heart to a man in the remotest part of Cornwall. I hope all fares well with this Robert Thornton and knowing you so well, I'm safe in the knowledge you are a good judge of character and will, hopefully, not let your heart rule your head. Please write soon, Jane, with your news. In the meantime you are ever in my thoughts and heart.

Yours, as always, Amy.

I clutched the letter to me. Dear Amy, how I could use her advice now and was I, quite contrary to her opinion, letting my heart rule my head over Robert? Only time would tell. I tucked the letter in a drawer and quickly prepared myself for luncheon and to face my grandmother.

Standing outside her bedroom door, I straightened the skirts of my day dress and touched my mother's amethyst brooch, which I treasured so much, hoping to gain some sort of courage from it. I need not have worried, for Grandmother was not as angry as I had expected. She sat by the fire and indicated for me to sit opposite her. I watched the large ring on her hand flash in the firelight.

'Jane, I am not going to admonish you further over today's unpleasant incident, but I wish you to tell me what has caused this strife between you and your aunt.'

She leaned back in her chair awaiting my answer.

'To be truthful with you, Grandmother, I am as perplexed as you except to say that today Aunt Laura intimated it was to do with my mother. This I cannot understand, as reading Mama's diaries she and Aunt Laura always seemed to be close except . . . '

I hesitated. Should I tell Grandmother what Mama had written in her diary before she left Pendenna?

'Except what, Jane?'

She leaned forward in her chair.

'Tell me, child, for I wish to know. You have not had the happiest of beginnings in life and my heart grieves for your mother for I should have helped her more. Now it is too late, but it is not too late to do the right thing for you. So tell me the truth, please, Jane.'

'Except for what Mama wrote in her diary,' I went on. 'She said Laura had no sympathy for the position she found herself in. It was as if Laura hated her. Why should this be, Grandmother? And why should Aunt Laura dislike me so?'

'I suspected at the time all was not well between my two daughters and wonder often if it could have been jealousy on Laura's part although

Laura was engaged to be married to Andrew. Your mama was always loved by everyone, including Andrew Trehaine. Laura was always possessive and domineering and Felicity went along with it because she was not of a quarrelsome nature. I can imagine that Laura could have despised your mama for getting herself with child and in some way escaping Laura's hold over her.'

'As we are being honest, Grandmother, is it possible that Aunt Laura is jealous of Robert and myself?'

'Oh, yes, dear, I do. She has had designs on him since the day he stepped through the doors of Pendenna Reach. I know Robert does not reciprocate Laura's desire for he has told me so, and Laura, too, but Robert is a gentleman and is polite and attentive to her for my sake and for the sake of peace, but your aunt now has you as competition for Robert's affections and if the affections towards you are realised she would undoubtedly resent you for it.'

'It would explain much and I must confess to not knowing how to deal with it.'

I sighed and Grandmother leaned forward and took my hand in hers.

'Tell me, Jane, for I need to know. Is there some affection between you and Robert?'

I did not know how to answer but the old lady coaxed it from me.

'Come, child, your mother was honest with me, though I could do nothing about the situation. I wish that I had, but for you, dear, I would do anything to further your happiness.'

'Yes, there is affection, and I believe it to be more than that on my part, for I am sure I love him.'

Grandmother let go of my hand and both her hands flew to her mouth.

'Jane, Jane, how happy you have made me but the question is, does Robert love you?'

She looked at me with expectation.

'I cannot say in all honesty for neither of us has declared a love for each other, but I am ever hopeful.'

'You must tell me, child, how this progresses for I had every hope of this as I have told you before.'

So saying she leaned back in her chair breathlessly.

'There has been enough excitement for one day and it must be time to go down for lunch.'

'And what am I to do about Aunt Laura for it worries me so?'

She again leaned forward and patted my hand.

'Ignore her unpleasantness, Jane, as I do. It is a pity she is this way but Laura has never been a happy girl. Ignore her.'

As we went down to lunch I thought how this advice was easier said than done.

Next morning, Robert, as good as his word, sought me out at breakfast to escort me to Granny Merriock's cottage. Why he thought I needed him I didn't know except I remembered my mother's words — *Granny Merriock came to the house today and told me to leave her grandson alone.* Was she hostile towards me, too, because my mother eloped with one of her own? Perhaps I did need Robert after all.

At my insistence, we walked. It was a dry, sunny day although the ground was waterlogged from weeks of rain. The ruts in the lane made by the carriage wheels made walking quite a trial and by the time we had arrived at the cottage my boots were covered in mud as were Robert's and my skirt was also mud-stained. We had spoken of everything from London to Pendenna, anything except that night alone together in the library. He steadied me several times on the way and his strong arm had encircled my waist, sending my pulse racing. As I made to step up the cottage path, Robert took my arm and drew me back to face him.

'Don't expect too much of this visit, Janie. I wouldn't want you to be hurt and distressed.'

So he thought as Aunt Laura. What did they know that I didn't but intended soon to find out?

'Thank you for your concern and support,' I said and squeezed the hand on my arm. 'This is something I have to do. She is my kinswoman.'

It was Robert who knocked on the door and it seemed for ever before it slowly opened to reveal Granny Merriock. Close to, she looked much older than I thought at first. Deep lines etched her cheeks and eyes, but her violet-coloured eyes were still sharp.

'Yes?' she questioned in a voice far stronger than she looked.

I glanced at Robert before I spoke.

'Mrs Merriock, I believe I am your great-granddaughter, Jane Merriock, your John's daughter.'

For what seemed like minutes, she looked me up and down.

'You are no great-granddaughter of mine. Please close the gate as you leave or the hens will escape.'

She spoke the words quietly but with such underlying venom I felt weak at the knees and tears sprung to my eyes.

Robert again took my arm and gently steered me towards the gate where I collapsed sobbing in his arms. Granny Merriock's words were so final I knew I could not argue with her. They had both told me, both Robert and Aunt Laura, but why? I vowed to find an answer.

The following morning, my eyes still red from weeping, I felt I needed to escape and have time to think so I decided to go for a ride on my own. After declining Molly's attempt to arrange my hair, I sent her down to Jack to ask him to saddle Amber for me. Before she left Molly turned at the door.

'It ain't my place to say, miss,' she said, 'but I see you've been crying. It ain't right you should be sad while I am so happy.'

'It's nothing, Molly. Now please run along while I get into my riding habit.'

When she had gone, I dressed myself in my riding clothes. Looking in the mirror, I tossed my long hair behind me, hardly recognising myself. Tapping my riding crop gently on my palm I made my way down the staircase and to my dismay Robert was walking across the hall with, of all people, Alan Lester. He stopped to look up at me, an unfathomable expression on his face, while Mr Lester gazed at me in what appeared disbelief, however Robert found his tongue.

'Where are you off to, Jane? And your hair . . . '

For once he was lost for words.

'I'm going riding, Mr Thornton. Jack is saddling Amber as we speak.'

'Allow us to come with you, Jane, for I can see you are distressed and it will only take us a moment to change.'

'No, thank you, but I wish to go alone. Good-day, gentlemen.'

I walked past them without a backward glance, heading for the stables. As I walked through the door I heard Robert call after me.

'But, Jane!'

I carried on walking, smiling to

myself. For once I had gone against his wishes and I felt quite pleased with myself.

As I rode towards Polgent, Amber picking her way expertly across the moorland, my hair blowing in gay abandon behind me, I had a momentary feeling that I was being followed but dismissed the thought, until I saw a man on horseback heading towards me. As he reined in his mount close to me, I could see with some pleasure that it was Jason Trehaine.

'Good morning, Miss Merriock. I hardly recognised you from a distance. May I hasten to add I don't mean to sound rude when I say that, for you do, in fact, look quite lovely and so much like your mother that for a moment I believed it was indeed her. You look sad, if I may say so. Is there anything I can do to help?'

'You are right, Mr Trehaine, I am sad and spent most of last night weeping. As to if you can help I do feel that I can confide in you but don't wish to burden you with my troubles.'

I smiled at him and when I looked at him again I thought how familiar he looked.

'Apart from my visit to your home some weeks ago, have we ever met before, Mr Trehaine? I thought when I first saw you that we had.'

'Indeed not,' he said most emphatically, then changed the subject rather quickly. 'Please, come back with me to Mannamead where we can talk and you can tell me what has upset you so.'

'Why, thank you, I would like that.'

So we spurred our mounts forward, riding along in a companionable silence. I felt so at ease with this man and trusted him implicitly.

Arriving at Mannamead, a stable-hand led Amber away but not before I fed her a sugar lump and caressed her face. The house looked so tranquil in the morning sun and the windows did indeed sparkle. Simms greeted us in the hall, relieving me of my riding cape and crop. We went again to the drawing-room where a cheery fire was already burning in the grate.

'Now, Jane, if I may be so presumptuous as to call you by your Christian name, tell me what troubles you that you weep all night.'

'It was Granny Merriock,' I said, plunging straight into the problem and I noticed Jason Trehaine was taken aback.

'Granny Merriock.'

He repeated the name as if he was in a trance.

'You have met with her, I take it?'

His voice was now back to normal but he still looked, for want of a better word, stunned. Why did this woman have such an effect on people? I set to wondering what Grandmother's reaction would be for I had not mentioned the name to her yet.

'Yes, I went to see her at her cottage yesterday afternoon. After introducing myself to her, she denied I was her relation and told me to close the gate as I left, but I know that she is my father's grandmother so why would she disown me in such a manner? I could not discuss it with her because I knew by her voice and the look in her eyes that was all she had to say.'

Jason Trehaine had listened to me and I could now see concern for me in his eyes. He stood up and looked out of the window for several minutes and then came back and sat down.

'Jane, there is much I could tell you but I feel this is not the right moment. Believe me when I say it is not Granny Merriock's fault. Trust me when I say that one day soon you will know the truth behind all this but I have to consult someone first before I dare lay bare to you all I know.'

His voice was steady and his words so sincere that I didn't doubt him but I was even more perplexed.

'And Aunt Laura?' I said, for maybe he could throw light on this also even though my grandmother had tried to enlighten me only yesterday. 'Why does she resent me so? Is it because of my mother? We had a confrontation yesterday outside the church and to say I am baffled by all this is very true. I'm beginning to feel unwanted here and I am seriously contemplating going back to London.'

'Your Aunt Laura is, and always has been, a very unhappy woman as I have told you before. She was always jealous of your mother.'

'Grandmother has told me this also, but I do not understand it. There is more to this whole problem than anyone is prepared to tell me but I trust you when you say you will enlighten me one day soon. Will it be here at Mannamead? Shall I call to see you one afternoon next week?'

'Yes, dear, it will be arranged, I give you my promise. Now let us have some lunch and weep no more, for we all love you and have your best interests at heart, no-one more so than myself.'

The next couple of hours I spent with Jason Trehaine were a tonic for me. His amusing conversation cheered me greatly and later that afternoon, when he escorted me back to Pendenna, the events of yesterday were firmly pushed to the back of my mind and I had every trust that this man had freed me from any doubt and puzzlement that I had in my mind.

While walking back from the stables after leaving Amber in Jack's capable hands, I encountered Robert with Alan Lester.

'Ah, Jane,' Robert said as he walked swiftly towards me, 'where have you been? Your grandmother missed you at luncheon but I did not tell her you were out riding alone.'

'So what did you tell her?' I asked.

'Only that you had gone riding.'

'Well, if you'll excuse me, gentlemen, I will go and find my grandmother.'

I made to walk on but Robert's strong hand caught my arm.

As I looked at him, his eyes looking into mine, he said, 'If the weather is kind tomorrow please ride with me to the Dancing Damsels. I wish you to look on them with happy thoughts. I have spoken with your grandmother and she has given her permission for us to ride alone.'

'But I vowed never to go there again. The whole visit filled me with foreboding and unpleasant thoughts.'

'You'll come with me, Jane, for I have something to say to you, something of great importance.'

As he spoke, he squeezed my arm gently, such a small gesture but it sent my pulses racing and I knew there was no going against his wishes.

'Very well, Mr Thornton, I will meet you here at eleven on the morrow.'

'Thank you, Jane,' he almost breathed a sigh. 'Till tomorrow then.'

So saying, he released his grip on my arm.

'Good afternoon, Miss Merriock,' Alan Lester said as they walked away towards the stables.

On reaching my room, I quickly changed from my riding habit to a day dress. Molly had lit a fire so it was fairly warm after the chill of the November day and the flames danced, casting their light across the walls, creating eerie orange shadows. As I pinned my mother's brooch to the pleated frill of my dress I thought of Robert's words and was more than curious to know what he wanted to say to me, but that would have to wait until tomorrow, for now I must seek out my grandmother. I guessed she would take me to task for missing luncheon.

I found her in the drawing-room, sat by the fire, looking very alert and full of expectation.

'Why, Jane, dear, sit opposite me so I can talk to you.'

Doing as I was bid, I seated myself.

'Apologies for my missing lunch.'

'Never mind about that,' Grand-mother interrupted. 'I've far more important things to talk about. I must tell you, dear, I have invited Mr Trehaine to dinner tomorrow evening and he has graciously accepted.'

My first thought at this news was that

Jason Trehaine had not mentioned this to me and idly thought this must be a surprise, which indeed it was.

'It is many years since a Trehaine has entered this house, let alone dine here, so we must make him welcome, Jane.'

'It will be a pleasure to do so, for I like Mr Trehaine very much, and how does Aunt Laura feel about this?'

'She doesn't know yet, but I will tell her later. I'm hoping it may lay to rest some of the ghosts which are haunting my daughter. Now, Jane, that brings me to something else which I wish to say, regarding that unfortunate incident outside the church.'

'Apologies for that, too, but I am quite perplexed as to why Aunt Laura should have been so spiteful to me.'

'I want you to tell me what the argument was over, Jane, and the truth, please, for the truth will out in the end, dear, and you would not want to lie to your grandmother.'

As she spoke, she looked me in the eyes. Hers were shining and held mine with determination and I knew I could only tell her the truth.

'It was over Granny Merriock,' I said quite boldly, at which her whole expression changed to one of fear and the eye contact was lost.

'Jane, I want you to tell me what you know of Granny Merriock.'

Her voice was strong.

'I only know that she is my paternal grandmother and for some reason disowns the fact, for I have visited her cottage and she practically closed the door in my face. Robert was with me.'

'What has this to do with Laura?'

'I saw Granny Merriock in the congregation on Sunday and tried to catch up with her as she left the church. Aunt Laura followed me, anxious to see the spectacle our meeting would cause. And as I told you, quite truthfully on Sunday, Aunt Laura was so spiteful to me and said she disliked me because I am my mother's daughter. To be honest, Grandmother, I can understand none of this. Granny Merriock disowns me, Aunt Laura seems to hate my mother and now me because I am her daughter. I spoke with Jason Trehaine today and he has promised me he will enlighten me very soon. There, now you have the truth of the situation. I am sorry but none of this is my doing and yet it seems somehow to have something to do with me. The question is, what?'

I bowed my head in my hands and started to cry quietly. I felt my grandmother pull me towards her, her arms around me. For some minutes I rested against the black taffeta and then drew back. Grandmother handed me a white lace handkerchief.

'Dry your eyes, Jane, and weep no more. You are indeed the innocent party in this situation which amounts to a charade and I will see that the whole unpleasant situation is brought to an end but I have to speak to someone first.'

At these words, I looked with surprise at her.

'But that is what Jason Trehaine said to me only today. It is you and he who have to speak together, isn't it?'

She did not answer me.

'Isn't it, Grandmother?'

In a weary voice she answered, 'Yes, my child. Jason Trehaine and I have to speak together.'

So saying, she laid her hand across mine, her ring sparkling in the firelight.

10

To say I spent a restless night is true. Thoughts of what Jason Trehaine and Grandmother had to speak of whirled around in my head and I came to many conclusions, probably none of them the correct one.

As I lay in bed I could see by the light on the curtains that it was a pleasant morning. I lay there, waiting for Molly to bring my breakfast while I thought of this morning's ride with Robert and wondered what it was he was so keen to say to me.

As usual, Molly was her cheerful self and busied herself preparing my bath and clearing the grate to light a fire. This morning I felt in a sombre mood and chose my dark riding attire. I let Molly arrange my hair, not wishing to displease or outrage Robert today. At this thought I smiled to myself. Had I really outraged the unconventional Robert Thornton yesterday? With some amusement I realised I had. Suddenly I felt better and now looked forward to my ride with Robert, alone. Grandmother had not mentioned it yesterday but I took it to be true that she had given her approval. Robert was many things but not a liar.

As I pinned my mother's brooch to the high neck of my white blouse, Molly draped the riding cape around my shoulders. Putting the finishing touches to my attire with my silk top hat, which I loathed, I was ready to face Mr Robert Thornton. As I approached the stables I could see he was already there. I could see Jack held Amber ready for me to mount.

'Good morning, Jane,' Robert said as I neared the stables. 'The weather is in our favour for November. It is a lovely day. How lucky we are.'

He was smiling and obviously in good humour.

'Indeed it is a nice morning. Even the

sea is calmer and not thundering on the shore.'

As I spoke, Robert's hands encircled my waist as he lifted me expertly into the saddle. His eyes met mine and I felt the colour rising in my cheeks and looked away quickly, thanking Jack, to cover my confusion. As we set off little did I know what confusion I would be faced with that day.

Robert rode beside me, reining his horse to keep pace with Amber and myself. As we passed Granny Merriock's cottage, Robert leaned across and gently laid a hand over mine.

'Think nothing of it, Jane, for today at least.'

I smiled wistfully back at him. Seeing the church tower in the distance brought to mind the unpleasant incident with Aunt Laura on Sunday and the conversation with my grandmother yesterday. Robert must have observed the solemn look on my face as he reined in our mounts.

'I want you to be happy today, Jane.

Clear all other thoughts from your mind for today is for you and me,' he said.

These words cheered me for wasn't this what I wanted, to be alone with this man whom I loved? Thoughts of him had filled my days since meeting him and our secret time in the library was the sun in my heart. Each time I recalled it I could still feel his lips on mine.

As we reached the field and the Dancing Damsels, Robert lifted me down from Amber. Instead of letting me go he pulled me to him and I could feel his heart beating fast. As he looked down at me I could feel myself trembling. I was alone with him, far from any other being and yet I trusted him.

'Janie, I love you,' he said in a burst.

The words came so suddenly from him I was taken aback.

'Why, Robert I . . . '

'Don't say anything for the moment, let me speak. I love you and please believe me when I say I have never said this before to anyone. I believe I have loved you since the moment I saw you at the railway station. I want to be with you always, to look after you and protect you. Janie, I want you to be my wife and I pray you can love me, too.'

As he released me, his words rang in my ears. His words had stunned me for I had thought of everything but this and yet it was what I desired. But what of Laura? Grandmother had assured me there was nothing between them but I had witnessed the scene in the woods that day, both of them close together somewhat intimately to my keen eyes. All these thoughts ran through my mind in seconds.

'Speak to me, Janie. Was I wrong in thinking this is what you wanted? Was I wrong to assume you felt about me as I feel about you?'

I turned away from him and stroked Amber's nose, catching sight of the ring of tall grey stones.

'Speak to me, my only love.'

His voice was full of urgency and imploring. I had to find the right words. To say the wrong thing at this moment could jeopardise any future I might have with this man, the man of my dreams. I turned to face him once more.

'You assume right that this is what I'd hoped for and that my feelings for you are different to anything I've experienced but . . . '

'But what, Janie?' he interrupted.

'What of Laura?' I asked softly.

'What about Laura? What has this got to do with your aunt? It is you I love and wish to marry. How could this in any way have anything to do with Laura?'

I could see he was exasperated.

'Have you forgotten the day I saw you together in the woods? Your hands were holding her arms and you were both so close you couldn't have got a taper between you. What have you got to say about that? Before I can think of marrying you I have to know what happened that day.'

Robert took my arm.

'Come, Jane, let us walk to the stone circle. Calm yourself while we walk and I will offer you an explanation. Put your arm through mine.'

I did as I was bid and we walked across the muddy ground. Robert was right, the stones did not hold me with such foreboding today. Robert leaned against one of the age-old stones, the sun falling on his face.

'I've been here a few times with my friend, Alan, and vowed I would propose to you here. It's an earthy place, far away from balconies and drawing-rooms and I wanted you to remember it always, but it hasn't gone as planned, no indeed not. I had hoped after our encounter in the library you had forgotten that day in the woods.'

'But how could I, especially on such a momentous occasion as you pledging your love for me?'

'I want you to trust and believe in me, Jane, that there is no attachment, or ever has been, between your aunt and myself. Please believe me, it was purely innocent the day you saw us in the woods but at this moment I cannot tell you why we were together.'

'Why not when you have asked me to become your wife?'

'Trust me on this, Jane.' His voice was firm. 'All I can say is that until I find the priest's hole I cannot tell you.'

'The priest's hole?' I uttered in astonishment.

'Yes. That small part of Pendenna Reach is very important to this conversation we are having now.'

'I think I may know where it is,' I offered.

Robert was suddenly very alert.

'You think you know, when Alan and I have scoured the house from top to bottom?'

'Did you try the nursery?'

'Why do you say that?'

'It was something Nora Blackstone said to me one day, that there was such horror to be found in these walls and that it was in the nursery.'

'We have to get back to Pendenna, Janie. This is important. Not so important as my proposal to you today but we will keep that in abeyance for a day or two. It will give you a chance to think it over. I realise it must have been a shock to you.'

'It was that, to say the least. I will think it over and I trust you also.'

'Now smile and let us hope you have opened the door to an age-old mystery.'

He dropped a kiss on my brow.

On reaching Pendenna, I made my way to my room to prepare for luncheon. I realised I was trembling and my legs felt weak. The events of the morning had been so unexpected I could hardly believe my good fortune. As I stood by the fire in my room, warming my hands, I reached idly to my mother's brooch at my throat and unclasped it. My hands were trembling so much that I dropped it and it fell to the grate. To my dismay, I saw that the gold backing had come apart from the stone. Gently I picked it up and looked at the opening in the back, behind the stone. To my utter amazement, Jason Trehaine's image was staring back at me!

I sank back in the chair by the fire clasping the brooch in my hand. Again I looked at the picture to ensure I was not mistaken. It was definitely Jason Trehaine as a young man. His age had not really altered him. Then I read the inscription on the back of the brooch — **I adore you for ever**. So it had been Jason Trehaine who had given my mother the brooch which she wore every day from as far back as I could remember. But why?

A dozen questions tumbled through my mind. I thought of Mamma's diaries and I stood up, an astonishing thought coming to me. He looked familiar because I was like him. At this thought, I ran to the mirror and stared at my reflection in the glass. I always thought I looked like my mother and had nothing of John Merriock's fair looks, now I knew why. Realisation dawned on me, and I truly believed that Jason Trehaine, of Mannamead, was my father.

A medley of thoughts ran through my head — my mother and father not sharing a room; Mamma's sadness each time she spoke of Pendenna, which was often; the love she mentioned in her diaries was not for John but for Jason. I recalled her words, my beloved will know what to do, and what did they do? How did I come to be brought up believing John Merriock was my father? I had seen their marriage certificate.

I had to have some answers. Then I thought of Granny Merriock saying, 'You are no great granddaughter of mine.'

She knew I wasn't her kin. Who else knew apart from my true father? My thoughts flew to my grandmother. She, too, must know the truth. I was so desperate to hear the truth but I must think about this, mull it over in my mind and not be hasty. I knew in my heart I was right. It explained so much.

I looked once more at Jason Trehaine's picture and gently closed the back of the brooch. To my relief it was not broken and I could see now how the back opened. How many times over the years had my mother opened this and gazed with longing at my father, my real father. I must be Jason Trehaine's only child. Recalling the day I first visited Mannamead, the picture of his wife came to my mind, and he had said she had died of consumption. And the paintings by John Merriock — what were they doing at Mannamead? He said he bought them as John Merriock was a good friend. Had they really been friends? I had to know what happened in the year of my birth and believed it was my true father who had all the answers.

It suddenly dawned on me that this evening he would be a guest at the Pendenna dinner table. Could I face him with composure, knowing the truth? I could do it, I had to, but for now I must keep silent until the time was right. Molly appeared while I was mulling these thoughts over in my mind.

'Have you had lunch yet, miss? Your grandmother is asking after you according to Cook,' Molly chatted.

'No, I haven't been down to lunch. I've decided to rest until dinner. The ride to the Dancing Damsels has tired me and I didn't sleep well last night.'

'No matter, miss, I'll bring you up some cold chicken and a nice pot of tea.'

Everything seemed so normal with Molly there but in truth everything was different. I picked at my lunch, drank my hot tea and then fell asleep, exhausted by the day's events. As I drifted off, I asked another question. Did Robert also know the truth?

I entered the drawing-room that evening purposely ten minutes late. As I stood at the door, I regained my composure and smoothed the skirts of my dress. I felt behind me to ensure the stiff silk bow was straight and then glanced down at the square, lace-trimmed bodice to which was pinned my mother's brooch. I took a deep breath to be ready to face both Robert and Jason Trehaine.

They were all assembled when I entered, as I hoped they would be. Robert stood out. I had not even thought of his proposal since finding the picture in the brooch. I instinctively touched it to make sure it was securely in place. Robert and Jason had obviously been in conversation and I wondered again if Robert knew the truth. I felt as if I was looking at a play being performed. Everything and everyone felt unreal this evening.

'Miss Merriock, how nice to see you again.'

Jason Trehaine crossed the room and I studied his features carefully, trying not to make it obvious and smiling as he came towards me. There was no doubt about it, I looked like him. Grandmother was silent as she watched the scene enacted before her. What was she thinking? And Laura, did she know? She sat in silence, next to her mother, with a scowl on her face. What was the real reason she hated me so much?

All the while these thoughts were going through my head I tried to smile and act normally, accepting a drink from Robert as he looked in my eyes, conveying the secret of his love to me alone. I suddenly found myself tongue-tied.

'Where is Alan Lester?' I stammered.

'He left this afternoon bound for Somerset and more stone circles,' Robert enlightened me.

Then I set to wondering about Aunt Laura and the priest's hole. Why had she denied its existence when my mother had noted in her diary that they had found it? Had Robert looked for it that afternoon? As if in answer to my thoughts, Robert took me to one side, much to Aunt Laura's displeasure.

'Meet me at breakfast. I want you to come to the nursery with me in the morning,' he said quietly.

I glanced around. No-one had heard.

The whole evening was a strain. How I got through it without screaming out that I knew the truth I don't know, but little did I know that the whole truth was to be revealed next day when the secret of Pendenna would well and truly be out in the open.

11

Robert was seated at the table when I entered the dining-room next morning, quite an unusual occurrence as he normally took breakfast early and then went riding out on the estate visiting tenant farmers. He looked up as I walked in and I prayed he wouldn't mention the proposal of marriage today for I had other things on my mind, but I needn't have worried for he, too, had more immediate matters to attend to.

'Good morning, Janie. I hope you slept well.'

As I helped myself to bacon and scrambled eggs and poured myself some coffee, I thought briefly of the night I had just spent tossing and turning, my mind full of the events of the past few weeks, but I wasn't going to admit this to Robert.

'I slept well, thank you,' I lied

admirably as I seated myself opposite him and sipped the strong hot coffee with some relish for I thought it may go toward making me feel more alert.

'So, you are ready to face our exploration of the nursery?' He paused. 'Or maybe you have changed your mind.'

'Not at all. I am looking forward to it as I haven't yet visited this room.'

'Are you not a little afraid of what you may find?'

Robert smiled at me, such an engaging smile I could not help but answer truthfully.

'With you, I would not feel afraid anywhere.'

It was the truth but as soon as I had uttered the words, I regretted it for fear he might misconstrue them and con-clude the truth that I was jelly in his hands. Robert didn't answer but neither did he mock me. Instead he placed a strong hand over mine, the look in his deep brown eyes warm and sincere. In that moment I knew we forged an unspoken understanding between us.

'Have you told my grandmother of our plan to visit the nursery?' I asked.

'No, I would not want to worry her. In any event, we may not locate the priest's hole. I have looked at many books and found no mention of it.'

'My mother mentions it,' I offered, 'in her diary.'

He sat looking at me for seconds which in truth seemed like minutes.

'Does she say in this diary where it can be found?'

'No, only that she and Laura discovered it when they were younger.'

'So, you only have Nora Blackstone's word that it is in the nursery, which makes sense. It is a place no-one would think to look.'

Robert sat back in his chair and I knew he was anxious to start our search.

'No matter, Janie, we will go ahead as planned although we have little to go on. More coffee?'

'No, I am refreshed, thank you.'

So saying we both left the room. As we made our way through the hall and up the staircase I saw everything in a different light. With Robert at my side, things did not seem so dark and although the eyes of my ancestors followed our progress, even the portraits took on a new meaning and I realised till now I'd never taken the time to look at them with much interest. At the top of the stairs was a large portrait of a young woman and I realised it could be my grandmother.

I lingered to look a little more closely but Robert was going on ahead so I quickly caught up with him. We passed the schoolroom. I then caught the strong scent of lavender as we passed Nora Blackstone's room, consequently my thoughts were of her as we opened the door of the nursery. We stepped inside and, looking around, I gasped in surprise. Everything looked as if the room was still lived in. The two beds on opposite walls to each other were made up and covered in pink bedspreads. On one bed was a china doll similar to the one I had found in the schoolroom but not so well cared for and I assumed it to be Laura's.

The floor was of wood and highly-polished and in the centre, a large pink and white rug lay as if new. I recalled Nora Blackstone's words that the nursery was in readiness. I thought with some hint of pity that she must have tended this room for twenty years and my heart went out to her when I thought of how her Felicity would never come back nor sleep again in one of these beds. In one corner beneath the window was a large wooden dolls' house, the small figures and furniture still placed where my mother may herself have placed them all those years ago when she was young and carefree. Then I thought of Aunt Laura. At some time in her childhood she must have been gay and happy, too, and I set to wondering again what had changed her to the unhappy, uncivil, discourteous person she had become.

While I kneeled on the floor to look closer at the dolls' house Robert was tapping the light wood panelling with which the walls were covered. Would he find the secret chamber where Roman Catholic priests hid in the seventeenth century? Half of me hoped our search would be fruitless in view of the governess's words and I felt a little afraid until I looked at Robert's tall, dependable figure and knew he would take care of me.

I joined him at some panelling on the outer wall by the high window. He was obviously interested in one particular partition.

'See, Janie, the outer wall is five foot thick here, or thereabouts. Tap this panelling here.'

I did as I was bid.

'Now tap this panelling on the other side of the window.'

I moved across and indeed it made a different sound.

'Would you not agree the sound is somewhat more hollow on the right than on the left? And look, here the seam is thicker.'

I could sense the excitement in Robert's voice. It was as he said and I started to tremble involuntarily as I wondered what we might find. Robert carried on tapping and deduced the panelling sounded different to a height of five feet.

'But if this is it, how does one open it?'

I could tell frustration was creeping into his voice and manner.

'There must be a catch somewhere, but where?'

'What of the window recess?' I suggested, more out of desperation to please him than anything else.

'The window, yes, Janie, the window. Why didn't I think of it?'

He set to feeling the stone recess carefully. A cry escaped him.

'I think I've found it. Please, get me that stool Janie.'

I dragged the heavy, wooden stool over to him and he stood on it better able to see what he had discovered. Anxiously I watched him and waited.

'This is very rusty and will not give easily, but before I try to pull it I wonder which way the panelling will go. It won't slide, but swing, I think.'

He got down off the stool, pushing it to one side.

'Are you ready, my love?'

I murmured my agreement as he pulled and pushed the metal lever which I could now see was hidden in a crevice in the wall. After what seemed an eternity, there was a creaking sound and we could see the panelling swinging back slowly and we both stood together in front of it, watching it with disbelief. The hidden room which was revealed was small with only space for a man to sit. In the stone behind was a small slit which provided air. I heard the piercing scream before I realised it was I who screamed. Slumped against the wall was a skeleton! The clothes, although deteriorated, hung loosely on the frame and a man's pocket watch dazzled my horrified eyes as the light from the window opposite danced on the gold casing.

Robert pulled me to him and I laid my head on his shoulder, the comfort of his arms around me. All too soon he turned my face up to his, away from the horror.

'Come away, Janie, come away. We will have to inform the authorities.'

He gently coaxed me from where I felt transfixed.

'But who is he, Robert?' I managed to ask quietly, my sluggish mind suddenly springing back into action.

'I have a good idea, a very good idea,' he said quietly.

As he led me to the door, we both stopped in our tracks. Nora Blackstone stood in the doorway.

'So you've found him then? I saw her coax him in, you know, and shut the door on him. She's evil, that one.'

So saying, she ran from the room. Robert and I followed, his arm gently around me.

In a daze, I was led to the drawing-room. I was trembling from head to foot. Robert thrust a glass of brandy into my hand and ordered me to drink it. I did so under his watchful gaze and then he rang the bell. Fortunately it was Mrs Dobbs who answered.

'My, whatever is wrong, miss? You look as white as my sheets and you are quivering like one of Cook's jellies,' she said, aghast at how I seemed.

'She's had a terrible shock. I want you to stay with her while I send for the police and Jason Trehaine,' Robert said.

'The police, sir? My, whatever is amiss?'

'I'll tell you all too soon, Mrs Dobbs, but for the moment keep Miss Merriock calm.'

'Why, yes, sir.'

By the time Robert returned, I had almost stopped shaking and felt somewhat calmer. The brandy had obviously worked. Robert ordered Mrs Dobbs to fetch my grandmother and Aunt Laura.

While we waited for them to join us, I asked Robert the question burning in my mind, as the scene we had witnessed in the nursery swam before my eyes.

'Who do you think it was, Robert?'

There was a long silence before Robert spoke.

'I think, my love, it is Andrew Trehaine, but that theory can only be verified when Jason Trehaine arrives.'

My hands flew to my mouth, the whole horror of it all dawning on me.

'And when Nora Blackstone said she saw her coax him in and close the door she meant . . . '

I could hardly utter the next words.

'Aunt Laura! Oh, my goodness! But why?'

'Don't distress yourself, dear, but it does look rather that way.'

Jason Trehaine arrived before the police and Robert took him up to the nursery. I wanted to join them but Robert wouldn't hear of it. My grandmother and Aunt Laura joined me in the drawing-room in the meantime, but I was sworn to secrecy not to say anything. Robert wanted to tell them himself.

'What is the matter?' Aunt Laura complained as she sat opposite me. 'I hate being disturbed while I'm reading in the library. What is the matter with you, Jane? You look as if you've seen a ghost.'

'Maybe I have,' I couldn't help uttering as she looked at me with such contempt.

'Don't start, you two,' Grandmother interrupted. 'My morning nap has been disturbed but I'm not complaining, nor should you, Laura. Robert wouldn't send for us for anything other than for a good reason.'

We sat in silence, waiting for Robert and Jason Trehaine. I still felt very confused about thinking of him as my father. My thoughts kept returning to the scene in the nursery and I realised with some sense of horror and disbelief that the poor man, whoever he was, had probably been incarcerated all my life.

When Robert and Jason entered the room we all turned to look at them, all of us in expectation, for different reasons. Jason Trehaine was looking shaken and Robert poured him a brandy, telling him to sit down. He sat in a high chair by a small, polished table, quite distant from the rest of us.

'What is this all about, Robert, and why is Mr Trehaine here? I need to get back to my nap, not that I will get back to sleep now,' my grandmother said, leaning back in her chair and yawning.

'I'm sorry, Mrs Pendenna, but I have some news which will shock you.'

Robert sat next to me as he spoke, opposite Grandmother and Aunt Laura.

'There is no easy way to say this, so I will come straight to the matter in question. Jane and I found the priest's hole this morning, in the nursery.'

Robert's eyes shifted from my grandmother to Aunt Laura who had suddenly sat up straight.

'I'm afraid to have to tell you that in the priest's hole, we found human remains. Mr Trehaine has identified a pocket watch as that of his brother, Andrew Trehaine.'

Aunt Laura stood up and went to the window, wailing. My grandmother, suddenly alert, had paled visibly but with great dignity said, 'Thank you, Robert.'

Robert went to pour another glass of brandy which he handed to my grandmother. She sipped at it, not looking at anyone.

'And do we know how poor Andrew came to be shut in a priest's hole?' she asked quietly.

'I have an idea but would like Mrs Dobbs to fetch Nora Blackstone.'

'You don't think it was Miss Blackstone? Surely not.'

My grandmother found strength in her voice and she glanced around at Laura who was still stood looking out on to the terrace.

'Laura, have you anything to say

about this? Come here and talk to me.'

Aunt Laura walked slowly towards us, her face expressionless but her eyes glittered with some emotion I could not identify. When she spoke she seemed in control of herself.

'There is no need to fetch Nora Blackstone. It was I who lured Andrew to the priest's hole and shut the door on him for what I thought was for ever.'

Her voice was rising and a sob escaped her lips. Although my grandmother must have been distraught at this revelation, she spoke quite calmly as if speaking to a child.

'And why did you do this, Laura?'

'Because he was to marry me but he loved her, Felicity, my own sister.'

Laura was now losing control as she faced me.

'She was pregnant with his child. Yes, Jane, Andrew Trehaine was your father!'

She screamed the words at me with such venom and hatred that I shrunk back in my seat.

'This is not true, Laura,' Grand-mother said with a firm voice. 'Why should you think this?'

Laura turned to her mother.

'Because I saw them in the woods together. They were walking close and were laughing, laughing at me no doubt, and when she told me she was with child, I knew it was Andrew's. How I hated her, and him, but she would never have him. I saw to that. But no-one will punish me for it for I have been punished enough over twenty years. I thought I could find love again with Robert, until she came on the scene!'

She looked at me once more.

'You are no better than your mother, stealing my man. I have never had any happiness and never will.'

I felt almost sorry for her, but her next action took us all by surprise. She suddenly ran to the door and before Robert or I could catch up with her, she had picked up the skirts of her green dress and was halfway up the staircase.

Robert shouted after her and I followed him. To my amazement, she fled to my room and as Robert and I reached the door it was too late. She had already reached the balcony and jumped.

My heart was pounding but while Robert sped back downstairs, I stepped out on to the balcony. I could see Aunt Laura's crumpled body lying on the ground below, her skirts spread around her. Even as I looked, Robert appeared and bent over her poor, broken body. As he looked up at me, I knew she was dead.

12

Aunt Laura and Andrew Trehaine were both buried in the family crypt in Pendenna church. It was a sad day, especially for my grandmother who had now lost both her daughters.

'But I have you, Jane,' she said to me after the funeral, hugging me to her.

The police were told the whole story and there were enough witnesses to verify that Aunt Laura had admitted to shutting her betrothed in the priest's hole. How sad, I kept thinking, that she was such a jealous woman to the extent that she would murder the man she loved, and no wonder Nora Blackstone was so deranged after what she had witnessed.

She had loved her two girls, Laura and Felicity, enough to keep silent all those years. Grandmother had spoken with Nora and now coaxed her to come downstairs more. Daisy Dobbs had kindly taken the governess under her wing and they took tea together every day. When the days were warmer, it was hoped that Nora would walk in the grounds of Pendenna again, but only time would tell.

The day after the funeral, two weeks before Christmas, in no mood for riding, I asked Jack to take me in the pony and trap to Mannamead. It was time I talked to Jason Trehaine. Simms opened the door to me and offered his sincere condolences. I was dressed in black out of respect for Aunt Laura. Grandmother had told me I only need wear it until Christmas Eve.

As I stood in the drawing-room waiting for Jason Trehaine I could feel the butterflies in my stomach and I was still wondering how I was going to broach the subject, but there was no need.

As he walked through the door and looked at me he said, 'You know, don't you, Jane?'

'That you are my father? Yes, I do, but how . . . '

'It was your manner the evening I dined at Pendenna. You kept touching your mother's brooch as you looked at me.'

I touched it now, for it was pinned to the neck of my dress.

'Seat yourself, Jane, and tell me how you found out.'

'I dropped the brooch that very day you came to dinner and I saw your picture. Everything suddenly fitted together, but I need you to tell me why my mother married John Merriock even though she was carrying your child.'

'It is a long story, Jane, but I will try to simplify it for you. Your mother and I fell very much in love but I was engaged to be married to Charlotte Trevellyan. It was a long-standing engagement, a match secured by my parents and one just didn't thwart one's parents in those days. When your mother found out she was with child, we both panicked. John Merriock was a good friend of mine and had always secretly loved your mother.

'I confided in him and he agreed to go away and marry Felicity, bringing up my child as his own. We hoped that when the child was born, your grandparents would welcome them back to Pendenna but Morgan Pendenna refused to have anything to do with his daughter, grandchild or the penniless artist she had married. I was at my wits' end for I knew that I would probably never see my beloved or my little daughter.'

He paused, his voice breaking a little.

'And what of the brooch which my mother wore each day?' I queried.

'On our last meeting, the night before your mother left Cornwall, I gave her the brooch with my image inside it so she would never forget me or the fact that I adored her.'

'And the paintings?'

'To make John feel better, I bought them to pay for their house and your schooling. I vowed you would be brought up in the manner I envisaged and that you and your mother would want for nothing. Jane, believe me when I say that I have lived in torment the past twenty years and when I heard your mother and John were dead, my first thought was to come and fetch you but at that time you would not have understood. I pray you understand now.'

He leaned across and took my hand.

'Yes, I do understand. In the past couple of weeks, despite all that has been happening, I have given it all much thought and you have now made clear to me the whole story. You were going to tell me anyway, weren't you?'

'I was but I had to speak with your grandmother first and I never got the chance, what with Andrew being found in such a shocking way and your aunt's death, but now you have come to me for which I am so thankful.'

'It was because of Granny Merriock you were going to tell me, wasn't it?'

'Partly that and I knew you would eventually fit things together, as indeed you have done.'

'And what of Granny Merriock?'

'She knew. John had told her and she never forgave him for what he did. I knew that if you ever met her something would be said. Can we now forget all this and work on forming a relationship?'

'We won't have to work very hard at it. I liked you the very first day I met you and I feel I know you so well.'

As I spoke, he pulled me to my feet and drew me to him.

'Ah, Jane, I thank God that I can at last call you daughter. And Jane,' he said as he put me at arm's length, 'promise me that when you fall in love, you will never let him go.'

'I promise,' and my thoughts turned to Robert.

No, I would not let him go, and after Aunt Laura's supposition when seeing Andrew and my mother in the woods, I realised how wrong she had been and how wrong I must be also. I knew I could not jeopardise a relationship for such a supposition.

As I made my way from Mannamead, my heart was light and I knew that I must seek out Robert and tie up the last loose ends. He was in the library when I found him and my thoughts turned back to the other occasion when I found him there. It seemed so long ago now. He looked up as I closed the door behind me.

'Jane, what a pleasure.'

'Ask me again, Robert,' I said and he looked perplexed. 'Remember the day at the Dancing Damsels? Ask me again.'

He stood up and came towards me. Gently, he took my hands in his and, bending towards me, his lips touched mine gently. What joy I felt.

'Will you marry me, Jane?'

'Yes, oh, yes, I will marry you. I love you with all my heart and will never let you go. I will adore you, for ever.'

We do hope that you have enjoyed reading this large print book.

Did you know that all of our titles are available for purchase?

We publish a wide range of high quality large print books including:
Romances, Mysteries, Classics
General Fiction
Non Fiction and Westerns

Special interest titles available in large print are:
The Little Oxford Dictionary
Music Book, Song Book
Hymn Book, Service Book

Also available from us courtesy of Oxford University Press:
Young Readers' Dictionary
(large print edition)
Young Readers' Thesaurus
(large print edition)

For further information or a free brochure, please contact us at:
Ulverscroft Large Print Books Ltd.,
The Green, Bradgate Road, Anstey,
Leicester, LE7 7FU, England.
Tel: (00 44) **0116 236 4325**
Fax: (00 44) **0116 234 0205**

Other titles in the
Linford Romance Library:

VISIONS OF THE HEART

Christine Briscomb

When property developer Connor Grant contracted Natalie Jensen to landscape the grounds of his large country house near Ashley in South Australia, she was ecstatic. But then she discovered he was acquiring — and ripping apart — great swathes of the town. Her own mother's house and the hall where the drama group met were two of his targets. Natalie was desperate to stop Connor's plans — but she also had to fight the powerful attraction flowing between them.

FINGALA, MAID OF RATHAY

Mary Cummins

On his deathbed, Sir James Montgomery of Rathay asks his daughter, Fingala, to swear that she will not honour her marriage contract until her brother Patrick, the new heir, returns from serving the King. Patrick must marry. Rathay must not be left without a mistress. But Patrick has fallen in love with the Lady Catherine Gordon whom the King, James IV, has given in marriage to the young man who claims to be Richard of York, one of the princes in the Tower.

ZABILLET OF THE SNOW

Catherine Darby

For Zabillet, a young peasant girl growing up in the tiny French village of Fromage in the mid-fourteenth century, a respectable marriage is the height of her parents' ambitions for her. But life is changing. Zabillet's love for a handsome shepherd is tested when she is invited to join the La Neige household, where her mistress, Lady Petronella, has plans for her grandson, Benet. And over all broods the horror of the Great Death that claims all whom it touches.